VAMPIRE DESTINY

////

J.R. RAIN
&
MATTHEW S. COX

THE VAMPIRE FOR HIRE SERIES

Moon Dance
Vampire Moon
American Vampire
Moon Child
Christmas Moon
Vampire Dawn
Vampire Games
Moon Island
Moon River
Vampire Sun
Moon Dragon
Moon Shadow
Vampire Fire
Midnight Moon
Moon Angel
Vampire Sire
Moon Master
Dead Moon
Lost Moon
Vampire Destiny

Published by
Crop Circle Books
212 Third Crater, Moon

Copyright © 2020 by J.R. Rain

All rights reserved.

Printed in the United States of America.

ISBN: 9798636057024

Chapter One
Way Too Fast

Vigilance and I are old friends.

Maybe even more than 'friends.' We started dating when I was real young, like nine. My parents didn't exactly take the best care of my siblings and me, so I had to keep my eyes open. Sure, lots of kids had it *way* worse than us, but it still kinda sucked. Mom and Dad never did anything actively bad to us. Mostly, they ended up being too high, busy, or lazy to take proper care of us. When he worked, Dad always seemed to end up with jobs where he'd have to spend long stretches of time away from home. He didn't open up his hippie natural products store until right around my senior year in high school.

Is it sad I have no idea if the place is still even open? It's been a shamefully long time since I saw my parents, but things are into weird territory now. Not sure how well they'd handle seeing me looking more like twenty-seven than forty-five. Oh, heck. Who am I kidding? They wouldn't even notice. There's a reason I stopped smoking weed after college and only tried LSD once. Well, *two* reasons: Mom and Dad.

Most of the vigilance I needed at age nine involved not maiming myself by doing dumb things most kids' parents stop them from trying. Some of it also went to the nights I spent sneaking onto the big farm at the end of our street, about a half mile away. Can't remember the name of the guy who owned it; not sure I ever bothered to find out. These days, my only memory of the place is sneaking in at night among giant green plants taller than me to steal vegetables when our fridge had only beer in it. I mean, how hungry does a little kid have to be to *want* vegetables. Maybe it would've been better for all of us if I hadn't been so careful and gotten caught. Social services might've gotten involved.

Fortunately, I had Mary Lou to look after me, so my childhood still had plenty of 'kid time.' My sister's the one who had to grow up too fast. She basically turned into a mini mom taking care of me and our three brothers while Mom stared at her crystals, smoked pot, or tried to get people to buy whatever mail-order stuff she signed up to sell that month. I think they still have four cases of cosmetics from 1994 in a closet somewhere.

The need to stay vigilant worsened in my teens, as it does for every girl. Never walk anywhere at night alone, avoid dark alleys, and so on. Being a young woman alone in some places was much scarier than sneaking onto a farm to grab some carrots or whatever. However, to be fair, actual trained vigilance didn't start until I saw my dream of becoming a federal agent come true, even if I did only wind up working for HUD. It lacked the flashiness of the FBI or CIA, but even those two branches are seldom like what's shown in the movies. They have plenty of boring days, too—HUD just had more.

My kids kept me on guard from the day I had Tammy at twenty-seven. They've kept me vigilant well into my fort—well… it's complicated. Hi, my name is Samantha Moon and I'm a vampire—sorta. I used to be a fairly traditional vampire. Claws, fangs, drank blood, couldn't tolerate sunlight, didn't show up in mirrors, the whole shebang. I hated having fangs. Hated thinking about them. They made me feel monstrous. So I retracted them... pretty much permanently.

See, the universe has a strange way of making things come into being if enough people regard them as real. Say the word vampire to most people, and they'll picture a blood-drinking fanged monster that skulks around in the shadows, hiding from the sun. Anyway, some highly unusual crap went down, and I ended up at ground zero of a magical explosion so powerful it changed the fabric of reality.

At least, my reality.

Few people see the Earth as a magical place in the sense of real, actual magic. For centuries, this inhuman monster called the Red Rider had been hunting down witches or anyone with magical ability and murdering them to siphon their power. He'd been terribly effective at his job, which is why few people believed in real magic anymore. When I destroyed him, all that built up magic exploded—passed through me—and went back into the world.

Quite literally, my body served as a living filter for the magical realignment of the entire world. As best as I can tell, the universe, fate, maybe the big Creator himself understood how I felt about the monster I'd become and... stuff happened. Or, maybe in those few seconds where all the magic in the world briefly existed inside me, I'd found the means to subconsciously make myself less of a fiend.

I'm a different kind of vampire now, a psychic one. I 'drink' mental energy. No more fangs. My canine teeth aren't even abnormally pointy anymore. Also, the sun and I are back on speaking terms. Which is awesome. Yay! Beach time. Really did miss catching rays.

Anyway, as soon as Tammy was born, I needed to stay alert for anything and everything that could potentially hurt her. Things became exponentially more nerve wracking two years later when I gave birth to my son, Anthony. A person might say I let my vigilance slip one night when making the fateful decision to go out for a nighttime jog.

As if...

No way in hell could I have done a damn thing about the vampire who targeted me. Becoming an undead... and now a not-dead-but-not-human immortal has been a mixed bag. It's got good parts and bad parts. Kinda destroyed the nice happy family we once had. My former husband, Danny, couldn't handle what happened to me and ended up mentally cracking. He started off trying to find paranormal ways to either 'fix' me or kill the monster impersonating his wife. Danny's pursuit of black magic led to him getting involved with the wrong people and ultimately dying. He'd learned enough to become a quasi dark master, who's now taken up residence inside my son's head.

I grew up with three brothers. There's a certain age where boys go through changes, their bodies start doing certain things, and they begin trying to hide adult magazines in their rooms. With three brothers, imagine how carefully I needed to tiptoe around our old house to avoid seeing anything disturbing or disgusting. Danny and I had it easy: one son.

You'd think it would drive the boy crazy having his father renting space inside his mind, always there, always watching. Never any privacy. I'm sure Danny checks out and flies off to wherever dark masters go at night when their hosts are asleep. Then again, with the Void having now collapsed, perhaps dark masters (even semi-dark masters like Danny), can leave at will. I'd like to think Danny gives Ant *some* privacy, especially if our son got a girlfriend. There had been talk of one a few years ago, but obviously that fizzled out. Maybe my son does have one, but chooses to not bring her around? Doubtful. Tammy would know, and she would have teased him about it endlessly. Hmm... maybe he's not interested in girls yet. He knows immortals have unintended effects on mortals they get romantic with. Could be, he's still trying to figure out what, exactly, he's become before risking turning some innocent girl into a mind slave.

It's almost seven at night on a Tuesday. I'm on my couch watching *Judge Judy* shred this young woman who went on an internet date with a guy she ended up disliking so much she called his work to complain about him. Almost got the guy fired. Judge Judy let her have it. Then she let him have it, too. Why hadn't he paid for dinner? It was a date, dammit.

Neither of my kids are home, an increasingly common occurrence. We haven't really done the 'family dinner' thing in a while. Nowadays, it's a combination of microwave entrees or Hot Pockets whenever the kids have time. Sometimes, I'll cook food and Tupperware it so they can take it when they want. None of us are *trying* to avoid each other or make a statement by not being a 'nuclear family,' but it's just sorta ended up that way.

Anthony doesn't bother with sports or anything competitive physically. The universe can be a bastard. It wanted to kill my son when he was seven. I've learned souls incarnate into each lifetime with a specific lesson they need to learn or goal they need to accomplish before moving on. Apparently, Anthony Moon got his diploma by seven and the universe declared him ready for reincarnation.

I objected.

No doctor on Earth could've saved him from his mystery ailment. I cheated with alchemy and vampirism. Yeah, I made my little boy into a vampire—but, thanks to an enchanted medallion, cured it immediately. He spent less than a day as an undead. What is he now? We're still not entirely sure. The same way I share a consciousness and body with Talos, Anthony can borrow the form of an entity we've come to know as the Fire Warrior. Even as his normal self, he's faster and stronger than ordinary humans. My son's also one of the most honorable people I know. He refused to play sports once he realized he had an unfair advantage.

And he's going to be sixteen in a few months.

Worse, my daughter turned eighteen today. Having a November birthday always made her feel 'too old' for her grade at school, since we held her back one year, not wanting her to start kindergarten at age four. Most of her friends' birthdays fall between February and April, with one in May. They won't turn eighteen until next year. Except for Ankita, Renee, and Ari. All three are a year behind her, presently juniors.

She didn't want a party, being 'too cool' to invite friends over and have cake anywhere around her mother. Being insanely telepathic, she felt me crashing into sadness at the thought, so agreed to have a little 'non-party' with just myself and Anthony—and a cake—before going out with her friends. And yeah, no eighteen-year-old wants a birthday party like they had when they were little kids. She's growing up out from under me.

I watch the remainder of the *Judge Judy* episode through a blur of tears, thinking about my soon-to-be-empty house. Anthony's still fifteen (for a few months) but he'll be eighteen in the blink of an eye. Two years (and two months) is a respectable amount of time, but honestly, it feels like they were six and four only a few weeks ago. Okay, admittedly, my life had a *lot* of stressful stuff going on for the past fourteen years… so it seemingly passing in a blur is more than simple nostalgia at their childhood slipping away.

When Judge Judy is over, I do something reckless and stupid.

Danny made DVDs of home videos we'd taken of the kids throughout the years. I put on the one with Tammy's birthday parties and start torturing myself by watching memories. Three-year-old Tammy getting a face full of icing when she tried to blow out candles. The next clip shows her fifth birthday party. She's running around with this doll she'd begged Danny to get her for weeks. Then six-year-old Tammy drives the big battery-operated car we got her into Danny's shin. Ten-year-old Tammy freaks out because Danny got her a computer of her own, which we couldn't really afford. I didn't realize back then he'd been taking money from shady people to do shady things for them as a lawyer. We hadn't been as financially stranded as he acted, but the income had been undeclared. He didn't even tell me about it. No surprise. By then, he thought I was a monster. Forget him. The next video shows Tammy at eleven trying to keep a polite face when Danny's parents give her six months of dance class as a birthday present. My living room fills with party games and the ghosts of cheering, happy children who've all gone away. They've become non-cheering, moody teenagers.

I stare at the screen, watching Tammy at various ages, hating the universe because time exists. Why do my kids have to grow up and not need me anymore? Why can't I keep my little girl under my wing for the eternity I've been given to spend on this planet? I'm the mom. Tammy and Anthony are the children. Dammit! I want it to stay that way.

They can't grow up and go off on their own.

Head down, I sigh, sniffling.

Yeah. Unreasonable. Overprotective. Clingy. Kinda pathetic, honestly.

But normal.

Hey, at least I'm up front with being overprotective. It's okay for me to feel this way. I'm not always going to treat my kids like they're six. Somehow, some way, I'll find the strength to let them spread their wings and watch life carry them wherever they may go. I would have had to do it anyway if our world had remained normal.

Anthony... might be around for a while, though. Despite *possibly* being an immortal, he hasn't gotten stuck at seven. Had I left him as a vampire, he would have become a permanent child. Ugh. Without the ruby medallion to cure his vampirism, I... don't know if my heart would've let me do that to him. Anthony stuck at age seven—or lost forever? What a choice...

Knowing me, I wouldn't have thought about it in the moment and been focused completely on saving his life. Again, thank God for the Alchemist. His magical charm really came through.

A medallion once owned by my one-time father.

Only to be taken from him by Rand, the vampire hunter.

And given to me.

To then be used to save my son from an eternity of vampirism.

Only... to have my son evolve into something unknown altogether. Not too long ago, Danny had told me the angels had taken an interest in my son. He suspected they were training him while he slept, teaching him in his dreams. Training him for what, I didn't know. Not even my son knew. And Tammy couldn't find evidence of the memory in his mind.

But yeah, he's growing up at a normal rate, thank goodness. Is he going to have an ordinary human lifespan and rejoin the Origin once he dies, since his soul had likely been ejected from heaven the moment I turned him? Or would he grow to adulthood, then somehow stop appearing older... then live forever? Guess we'll find out. Can't say I would object to him being around for centuries. We're going to lose Tammy eighty, ninety years or so down the road. Gonna take a lot of willpower for me not to seek her out when she reincarnates.

I continue watching the DVD.

Tammy's birthday during my separation with Danny when he'd barely let me talk to them comes on next. The bastard had the party early in the day, knowing I couldn't be there because of the stupid sun. He'd barely let me have fifteen minutes on the phone with the kids at pre-scheduled times. My daughter looks depressed and angry. She keeps glaring at him with a 'why isn't Mom here?' glower. And Danny's parents gloating in the background pisses me off all over again.

Argh. I can't bear seeing her so angry-sad.

I skip to the next birthday. Maybe someday, I'll be able to watch this one, but too soon. It makes me want to pull Danny out of Anthony and punch him in the nose. Bad enough the anguish he put me through keeping the kids away from me, but seeing the same pain on Tammy's face is beyond the pale.

Maybe I shouldn't have put this video on. It's hard enough allowing her to grow up in my head. She's eighteen now. A legal adult. Worse,

I don't have to say or do anything. She always knows exactly what my feelings and thoughts are. Maybe she avoided a party because she didn't want me to spend the whole time crying and 'mourning' her childhood.

Deep breaths. I killed a version of the Devil. Handling my kids' growing up ought to be easy.

Speaking of my kids, Anthony should be calling me soon for a ride home. Ever since we got back from our European trip—wow, what a ride that was—he's been going to see Jacky at his gym three times a week or more. He's not working on becoming a boxer due to his unfair advantage, nor does he need to exercise. His body, like mine, has become something supernatural and doesn't benefit from training or working out. Anthony's going there primarily to spend time with Jacky, who's kind of stepped in as the grandfather my son never had.

We didn't have much (okay, any) real contact with my parents. While the kids *did* spend some time early on with Danny's mom and dad, those grandparents (predictably) took my ex-husband's side when we separated and helped him keep the kids away from me for a while. I'd like to say I'm better than allowing petty resentment to linger, but nah. Ever since I got them back, Danny's parents haven't been too welcome around the family. The kids asked to see them once or twice early on after they came home, so a few visits happened. Anthony gets on with them better than Tammy. Not sure if she's older, so she realized how they tried to turn the kids against me or she's more upset with Danny than she lets on.

But yeah, it's been a while, and the kids had no real grandparental influence.

Enter Jacky.

The supernatural stuff has gotten crazy to the point where I haven't had the chance to spend much time at the gym. Anthony mentioned Jacky's wife passed away roughly a year ago to cancer, and he didn't handle it well. Of course, being old school, the man would never admit he's depressed. His generation toughed through everything. Men couldn't admit to emotions, and so on. I think Anthony reached him on some level. The two of them have a sweet rapport damn close to grandfather/grandson.

Tammy's at her friend Veronica's house along with several other friends. She said something about Veronica's mom taking them to the mall or movie or some such thing, but mostly, they'd be hanging out at the house having a birthday non-party. Apparently, the phrase 'birthday party' sounded too juvenile for Miss Eighteen.

Speaking of her growing up, my brain decides to go off on a tangential worry about college. So far, it sounds like she definitely wants to go, even if she can't decide what to major in. As anxious as she's been about the whole application process, I've been equally anxious over if she'll go someplace close enough to keep living at home or end up in dorms somewhere. No point in me suggesting she stay local, at least for the first year to get used to college life before taking on the stress of having to live somewhere new *and* deal with a completely different experience.

She knows how I feel.

But, I also want her to make the decision for herself, based on what she wants to do. Sure, it will bug me if she goes far away, but it's not my place to live her life for her. Won't stop me from spending a few years obsessing over home videos of my kids, but I'd hardly be the only mother in the world to do it.

Sighing, I pause the video.

Okay, wow. This house is entirely too quiet.

I proceed to wander around, trying to dodge the ghosts of memories haunting me. Everywhere I look, *something* triggers a memory of the kids or even Danny. Am I going to be one of those crazy parents who leaves their kids' rooms exactly as they were when the child moved out as some kind of shrine to the past? Maybe. I'm definitely not going to convert their rooms to a yoga studio before their car is out of the driveway.

Most likely, I'll spend a few years being pathetic... then finally do something. Maybe I'll get a dog. Maybe I'll turn into a cat lady.

I'm too much of a mom to have an empty house. Hmm. I could always adopt another kid, or foster. The world's got plenty of orphans and not enough homes. Better to use my money helping someone feel loved and wanted than on fancy cars or boats. Question is, could I deal with getting attached to another child? Would it be fair to them to be pulled into my bizarre world? Sooner or later, any orphan I adopted would have to be let in on my secret. A foster kid I could keep in the supernatural dark, but adoption is going to require going all the way.

I'm forty-five (almost forty-six) and I still look like I'm under thirty. While I happened to be thirty-one at the time of the vampire attack, something about the process makes people prettier or younger. After all, vampires in most folklore are sexual beings who use charm and romance to find people to feed on. When he'd still been relatively friendly to me, Danny told me I looked twenty-seven. This one shopkeeper in Denmark thought Tammy was my little sister!

No one looking at us would *ever* believe I'm Tammy's mother. It's something the kids and I have already discussed. If anyone mistakes me for a big sister, they run with it unless it's a school administrator or someone important. Anyone who *needs* to see 'Mom' gets me and a dose of mental prodding to ignore how young I appear to be.

At least with Tammy being eighteen now, the need to have a parent around to sign stuff is pretty much gone. And Mary Lou could always impersonate me if need be. My sister's fifty-one now. I won't say she looks her age, but she definitely appears to be old enough to be Tammy's mother.

In far too short a time, Anthony will hit the big one-eight as well. He's already so big he's basically an adult except for his boyish face and relative immaturity. I say relative since he's like the most mature example of a teenage boy I've ever heard of… but he still finds farts hilarious. Do boys ever grow out of that?

I've never considered myself even the least bit vain. Still, I end up staring at myself in the mirror for a while, unsure how to feel about the face looking back at me. Looking exactly the same as I did a week after I became a vampire only makes the blur of the past fourteen years worse. It's as if I closed my eyes and my cute, adorable, caring four-year-old daughter and fearless little toddler son turned into grown-ups.

"Hey. At least mirrors work on me again." I make a stupid face at myself and walk out.

My wanderings eventually bring me back to the living room. As soon as I look at the couch, my head fills with memories of little Tammy snuggling up with me. She used to do it all the time whenever I came home exhausted, stressed, injured, or sick. At six, she stopped believing sitting next to me would magically cure whatever made me feel bad, but still did it.

I'm going to drive myself crazy living in an empty house, aren't I?

Need air.

Before I realize it, I'm outside jogging on the street, following my old route. The exact path that led me to my almost-death fourteen years ago: down Shady Brook Drive to the little spur connecting it to Lemon Street. I cut over the spur and jog past Lions field, running along a thin strip of trees separating it from the road. Lemon Street goes to the park entrance, opposite where Virginia Road cuts off to the right, a nice curving path around the woods.

Fourteen years ago, I'd come the same way, anxious about a HUD investigation, clueless what waited for me or how my life would change. Still not sure who the vampire was who initially attacked me. My sire, Jeffcock, interrupted him and turned my dying self into a vampire. Despite his efforts, Elizabeth still got me. No point wondering what the first attacker wanted. Somehow, it all probably played into Elizabeth's plan—and of course, my guardian angel being derelict in his duties.

But, as they say, there's a plan for that, right? Perhaps powers greater than a guardian angel breaking the rules and falling in love with the person they'd been charged to protect set things in motion. It's a romantic thought, but not sure it's a believable one. Seriously, who am I to warrant the attention of the universe?

When I reach the spot where the attack happened, I stop gazing around for a moment before staring at the tree the fiend threw me into. Tonight is quiet and peaceful, a gentle breeze slightly chillier than comfortable in only a T-shirt.

"Fourteen years," I whisper to no one in particular. "What a long, strange trip it's been."

My cell phone rings.

It's Anthony.

"Hey, kiddo."

"Sorry. I know it's a little later than I said I'd call. Jacky needed help with moving a bunch of stuff around and cleaning up. One of the heavy bags burst open so I helped him get it down and throw it out."

"Uh huh. And how did it burst open?"

"I think you know how it burst open."

"I think I do, too."

"So, yeah. I'm ready to come home now. Can you pick me up?"

"Of course. Be there as soon as I can."

"Cool. Thanks, Mom."

I smile. "On my way."

After hitting 'end call,' I teleport home and hop in the Momvan. This poor thing is on its last legs—or wheels. Danny and I bought it expecting to have two kids involved in team sports, having to schlep them around to soccer, football, baseball, gymnastics, dance class, karate, or who knows what. Weird how life turned out for us. Neither kid ever really got into organized activities. I never really became a soccer mom. Then again, I'd have been the mom on the sidelines watching the game other kids' dads called 'smoking hot.' And they would've been literal. Thanks to the sun, I'd have been gradually smoldering the whole time. Anthony briefly dabbled in sports at Danny's urging, but it soon became obvious how much of an advantage he had over other kids his age. He felt like he cheated and we (Danny and I) agreed to let him give it up to avoid attracting scrutiny to our strange, supernatural family.

The ride to downtown Fullerton doesn't take long. It's a bit of a gentrified area full of coffee shops, stores, restaurants, a few yoga studios, cute boutiques, and Jacky's gym. It's like the one working class guy hanging out at the Hipster bar. His gym hasn't changed in fifty years, the kind of place Rocky would've trained at.

Meanwhile, Anthony's too big for his age. He almost looks like a grown man with a mild steroid addiction. In a few years when his face catches up to his age, he could be intimidating if he wanted to. Heck, he could be scary *now* if he wanted to.

He hops in as soon as I stop. "Thanks, Mom."

"What, like I'm going to make you walk." I grin.

"I know, but..." He gives me a quick hug, as much as one can while sitting in the front seat.

"Did you eat yet?" I ask. "We could stop

somewhere on the way home."

He shakes his head. "Not yet, but it's cool. I can microwave something."

"Up to you."

Anthony is quiet for a moment as I drive, then looks over at me. "Mom, I'm kinda worried about Jacky."

"Oh?"

"He seemed a little off."

Even though I can't read my son's mind, it's obvious he's legitimately upset. "Should we go back?"

"Nah, he's not *that* bad. Just seems... different. Distracted." Anthony twirls his hand around as if searching for words. "Couple times, he kinda got lost in the middle of a sentence and forgot what he was going to say."

"He used to be a boxer. And he's getting old now. What's he, seventy-eight?"

"Seventy-seven I think..." Anthony picks at his jeans.

"I know it's hard to see."

"Yeah."

"He's basically your grandpa."

"Yeah, I guess."

I slow for a red signal. We're silent for a few seconds, sitting there at the light.

"Sorry I didn't bring you around my parents

and avoided your father's family whenever possible," I say, eyes downcast.

"It's all right. I understand why you did it." He takes a deep breath, letting his emotions settle. Like Danny, he's usually good at keeping his feelings off his face. "You don't really get along with your parents 'cause they were kinda crummy to you, and I know Dad's parents never liked you."

"Yeah… Mom and Dad weren't 'crummy' to us as much as had better things to do than pay attention to our existence." The light turns and I step on the gas, the Momvan unenthusiastically lurching into motion. Not sure if she's being sympathetic to my somber mood or needs to go back to the garage.

"That's being crummy," he says. "I mean, you kinda *died* and yet you still spent so much time with me and Tam."

Not sure if I should laugh or cave in and start sobbing. I end up sighing.

"Supposed to be funny." Anthony play-punches my shoulder. "Sorry."

"It's fine. I'm just having a melodramatic moment."

He grins. "Well, you *are* Tam's momma. Everything worth doing is worth doing melodramatically."

"Oh, brother."

"Hey, Mom?"

"Yeah?"

"I know you and Dad's parents never got along... how come?"

I fidget at the wheel. "Well, two main reasons. The big one was I grew up poor and they didn't think I belonged in the same social circles as their Danny. You know, a man who'd never had to go without shoes due to lack of money."

"Wow... you seriously didn't have shoes?"

"Yeah, for like a year and a half. Parents lied to the school and said I refused to wear them because of hippie religious BS or something. Mary Lou finally threatened to tell social services, so they got us some... and Clayton didn't wear them because he really was too much of a hippie."

Anthony chuckles.

"Second reason came down to them being religious. They *really* didn't like that I wasn't."

"I don't think shunning people is what Jesus would have wanted."

"Yeah... you're right." I sit there, not shutting off the engine, not getting out of the Momvan, staring at the garage door. Hmm. If the Devil exists because humans believe he does, then Jesus must be out there, too. Something to think about. And, hmm... I wonder what he's up to.

The *ping-ping-ping* of the door alert makes me snap out of my philosophical mental reverie.

"Mom? You okay?" asks Anthony, already out of the Momvan.

"Yeah." I shut the engine off and open my door. "Only thinking. We can order a pizza if you want."

"Cool. Yeah." He grins. "Awesome idea. Way better than microwave!"

Chapter Two
A Case of the Mondays

Nature has no shortage of opposing forces.

Cats and dogs. Spiders and bugs. Vampires and sun. Workaday people and Mondays.

I cheat, at least for the last two things since cats *and* dogs are both cool in my book. Spiders, bugs, and other creepy stuff never really bothered me. Unless you count black widows the size of VW buses that live underground in the desert. Long story.

It used to freak Mary Lou out when we were children and she'd see me playing with a spider or centipede, letting it crawl on my hand or arm. Usually, I'd end up putting it on my brother Dusk since despite being three years older than me, he'd always scream the way most people might expect a little girl to scream upon touching a spider. Mary Lou didn't find it as funny as I did.

Clayton was like me and loved bugs as a kid. He tended to wear them (and mud) more often than clothes. My eldest brother, River, on the other hand, didn't really like playing around much, especially as the victim of a prank. Don't really remember what I did to him for a laugh, but he stuffed me in this old washing machine we had in the backyard, and wedged the door. Took Mary Lou all damn day to find me. Yeah… I left him alone after that. River isn't what most people would call a 'nice guy.' Had some legal issues as a teen, ended up in jail from eighteen to twenty on a grand theft auto charge. Last I heard, he's been on the straight and narrow ever since, but we haven't spoken once since he left home.

As far as cheating goes, I'm a vampire who loves the sun and I work for myself. You might think being your own boss would allow me to not work on Mondays… but after a decade of being a private investigator working whenever I want, weekends kinda lost much of their significance. It's a bit like being unemployed, only with less free time. Along with weekends, the dreaded Monday doesn't really matter to me anymore. Waking up not feeling like going to work on a particular day means I don't go.

It's nice.

Even nicer post-inheritance.

In theory, the income from interest is enough to live on… more than I used to make at HUD. Staying in the same house rather than going bonkers on a big place or a move to a ritzy area means there's no *need* for me to work at all anymore. But… boring. Not to mention sitting around all day would leave me to spend hours obsessively worrying about Elizabeth and her crew of dark masters. Might get a new car—again a normal car, not something pointlessly expensive—as soon as I defeat my sentimentality toward the Momvan. She's almost a member of the family.

So, several things remain true in my life:

Tammy is still eighteen.

I'm still working as a PI.

Mondays are the inevitable aftereffect of a weekend.

Did I mention my daughter is no longer legally a minor?

I lean back in my chair and grab two fistfuls of hair. Get a grip, Sam. Kids grow up. They're supposed to. Mary Lou's oldest daughter Ellie

Mae is twenty now. She's up in Washington State going to college. My sister didn't flip out too much at her turning eighteen. Billy Joe's going to be eighteen in January. He's managed not to flunk out of high school and is poised to graduate this year. He's already got a job lined up with an electrician. No college for him—and I'm not saying that as a put-down. He'll be doing what he loves and making decent money while most kids his age are sinking into student loan debt that'll take them well into their forties to pay off.

My sister's youngest, Ruby Grace, is only sixteen and already taking college-level courses. She might even skip senior year of high school (graduating early) if the scholarship pans out. Of course, if it doesn't, I'm going to offer to help them out. It's the very least I can do for my sister after all the help she's given me over the years.

Yeah, I'm pathological about Tammy. Probably has something to do with me being immortal. Mary Lou didn't get all emo over her kids crossing the big eighteen because she's not going to be around to see them die of old age.

Three days after Tammy's eighteenth birthday, the world hasn't stopped rotating.

It's only me who feels like it has. Suppose I

should consider myself lucky since she hasn't thrown being an 'adult now' in my face as a defense for me telling her not to do something. Then again, it *has* only been three days. Still, our relationship is pretty decent. Guessing most parents would call me 'permissive,' but I think of it as trusting her. Also, she can read my mind, so she knows my feelings at any given moment. Yelling at her or asking her not to do something even once already feels like nagging since she's heard it passively before it leaves my mouth.

So weird. Anthony's overly mature and well-behaved for a boy his age. Tammy's off the beaten path, but still not the usual sort of teenager. I really would trust either one of them to be responsible on their own already, probably why I've been training myself to be the 'here if you need me, but I'll let you try flying first' sort of mom. My parents hadn't been permissive— they'd been oblivious. Short of something *way* dangerous, like the time Clayton found Dad's gun, they generally acted as if we didn't exist. And even then... True, Dad took the revolver away from the boy, but he'd never win parent of the year. He didn't realize Clayton was 'playing cowboys' until *after* my brother fired a shot into one of the appliances in the backyard.

No, I hadn't been in it at the time. Clay found the .38 when he was five. I'd only been three then. Don't remember it happening, only the story Mary Lou told me. It had been the first time she ever remembered our parents arguing. Mom was, predictably, furious, and freaked out. Dad? He'd been proud of Clayton for hitting the stove.

Remember me still doing the PI job to keep my mind off Elizabeth? Yeah, it doesn't work so well when I'm sitting idle in the office. At least my office is in the house, and I don't need to commute anywhere. My investigation business never wound up being profitable enough for me to rent a real storefront office downtown, but it let me keep the house and take care of my kids. Good enough.

The world has such a weird sense of irony. Now that I *can* afford to rent a downtown office, it's not necessary. My ceiling holds no answers as to what Elizabeth is planning or how I can get over my kids growing up. I'm not dumb. It's obvious *why* my emotions are all over the place. For the past eighteen years, my kids have been my *entire* world as much as possible. I'm not ready to go from being in a constant state of how best can I look after my kids to becoming the parent of adult children who don't need me around 24/7. Yes, there's quite a bit of simple nostalgia at missing them being cute and little, but it's really me being afraid of change.

What am I going to do with myself once they're both out on their own?

I lean back in the chair and let a long, slow sigh out my nose.

Maybe Kingsley will step in. Without the need to take care of two kids, I could accompany him on all sorts of trips. Visit the world and so on. Maybe sleep at his place more often. Something tells me Mr. Fancy Pants isn't interested in moving into my painfully normal suburban house. I'm not sure I'm interested in moving in with him either. Spent too many years being resentful of people who didn't have to wonder *if* they'd have food at any given moment to fully integrate myself into his world. I'd make a comment about how deeply childhood experiences shape the adults people become, but as far as I know, Kingsley grew up relatively poor. He crewed a fishing boat for a while years ago before deciding to become a lawyer. These days, he has no qualms about enjoying the finer things.

The phone rings, interrupting me thinking about if sufficient time spent as an immortal changes people. My immediate answer is, yeah probably.

Anyway, it's the PI phone, so I answer with, "Moon Investigations. This is Samantha."

"Hello. My name is Greta Adams," says a woman who sounds my age and worried. "I'd like to hire you to help me find my mother. She's missing and the police aren't having any luck."

"How long ago did you last hear from her?"

"Umm. Yesterday. Mom's a little... eccentric. Sometimes, she randomly goes places or wanders off, but this doesn't feel right. Given her history, I think the police aren't really looking too hard yet. They probably think she'll turn up on her own in a day or two."

I twirl some hair around my finger. "They said that?"

"No, not really. I'm guessing. The cops I spoke to didn't sound too worried. Guess they might be jaded."

"Could be. That twenty-four-hour wait thing is a Hollywood myth. All the cops I've known take missing persons reports seriously right away. It's possible in the case of an unimpaired adult where no signs of a crime have occurred they might not give it as high a priority as they would for a missing child or someone with difficulties."

"I understand. But there *is* a crime. Men with a van took her."

"Really?" I sit up in my chair. "Why would the cops not be prioritizing her disappearance then?"

Greta exhales hard. "Because it looks like Mom got in the van willingly. But I know her. Something's wrong."

"Witnesses described her getting in the van?" I ask.

"No, the security cameras recorded it."

"All right. I have room on my schedule. Why don't we meet somewhere to go over the details? Where are you coming from?" I ask.

"I'm in Corona. Mom lives in Beverly Hills."

My eyebrows go up. "Okay, Corona isn't too far. Straight shot down 91. Want to meet at the Starbucks off Green River by Brandon's Diner? Say in about an hour?"

"All right. I can do that. See you there. Thank you."

"On my way."

I take a few minutes to start a case file, then throw on shoes and head out the door. Hmm. The Momvan's looking a little long in the tooth. Maybe I shouldn't burden her with a ride to

Corona. Easy enough for me to get there without a car.

One of these days, someone is going to see me leaping into the air on angel wings. No one does today, though. If anyone ever saw me, it wouldn't take much effort to make them forget. My flight is uneventful and doesn't take anywhere close to an hour. Traffic is pretty light at 2,500 feet, and cops can't pull me over for breaking the speed limit up here.

A Taco Bell stands at the western side of the parking lot it shares with the Starbucks, the diner, and two gas stations. I come in for a landing by a thick row of trees separating the Taco Bell from an office building in the next lot—greenery makes for good cover—and walk to the Starbucks.

A Starbucks I know all too well. After all, a few years ago, a woman disappeared here, and I'd been brought in to help find her. Put it this way... I'll never look at these bathrooms the same again. 'Nuff said.

Being early, I have plenty of time to grab a latte before heading to the corner and sitting in one of a pair of wingback chairs on either side of a tiny, round table. This vantage point allows me to see everyone entering the place and briefly scan their thoughts. I'm not burrowing deep, merely looking for someone thinking about finding me. At about twenty-to-one in the afternoon, there aren't too many people popping in. Most who hit this Starbucks are either coming from the gas stations before getting back on the highway or walking over from the office building. The area's surrounded by a small enclave of residential development, though people who live there are no doubt at work now.

About eighteen minutes after I sit, Greta Adams walks in. She's pretty obvious even before I ping her brain, due to her worried, searching expression and how she first looks around at the seating area instead of the register. She's in her mid-thirties with auburn hair, wearing a fairly ordinary top and jeans. Doesn't seem wealthy nor struggling. Dolce & Gabbana purse, though. Between it and her mentioning Mom lives in Beverly Hills, I assume her mother's comfortable. Perhaps Greta is as well but, like me, doesn't feel the need to flaunt it.

I catch her eye and wave.

Somewhat confused, she approaches me. "Samantha Moon?"

"That's me." I stand and offer a hand. "Greta?"

She hesitantly shakes my hand. "Yeah. How did you recognize me?"

"Educated guess. You walked in here rather obviously looking for someone."

"Oh." She relaxes, half chuckles, and sits in the other chair.

I sit again, smiling at her. "No cyber-stalking involved."

"Had me worried there a bit, but maybe I shouldn't be. If you could've found out who I am so fast from a name, you can definitely find Mom." Greta hands me an eight-by-ten envelope. "Here's some information and a photo."

Nodding, I open the envelope to find a professional portrait photo of a sixtyish woman with short, silvery hair. It looks like the sort of photo authors stick in the back of their books or real estate agents post on tiny billboards. She seems kinda familiar. Probably resembles someone I met once. I'm sure I've never seen this woman before.

Papers behind the photo contain a long list of email addresses.

"What's this?" I ask, holding up the emails.

"It's an export from her website. Her fans, mostly. You know, in case one of them might have abducted her." Greta clasps her purse in her lap, fidgeting. "Like I said before, Mom is kind of eccentric and has been known to wander off before."

"Your mother has fans?" I raise both eyebrows, trying to think of a famous woman named Adams.

"Yeah. Not *too* many, though. But the ones she has are true fanatics. Ever hear of Zandra Adams?"

I stare at the photo. "She looks a little familiar, but the name's not ringing any bells. Sorry."

"It's okay. Most normal people don't know her." Greta manages a weak smile. "My mother is a writer/director. She's made, oh, about thirty-seven movies, nearly half of which she also wrote the screenplays for. Yeah, they're mostly B-films and some straight-to-video specials, but, like I said, she has a group of devoted fans, to put it mildly."

"Oh, wait... *The Vampire Fiona?*"

Greta nods. "Yeah. That's one of Mom's."

I grimace inside. Danny showed me that movie soon after my transformation. At the time, I'd thought it one of the cheesiest things I'd ever seen... don't remember much other than the main character was a vampire hunter who came off like Inspector Clouseau trying to do a Dick Van Dyke impression while ridiculous amounts of blood sprayed everywhere.

"It's okay if you didn't like it." Greta fusses at her hair. "I think the vampire stuff is nonsense too. Honestly have no idea why people are into it. Most of my mother's films are like that. Vampires, zombies, wizards, aliens… she doesn't make anything *real*. Probably why she never hit it big."

"It's not everyone's cup of tea, but there are lots of people who love those sorts of stories. Vampires are pretty popular."

Greta half shrugs. "Yeah. I know. She's doing well enough. She doesn't have millions of fans, but the ones she does have are pretty loyal. They've been emailing her for years, asking for a sequel to that *Fiona* movie. Mom wants to make one, but she hasn't been able to sell a studio on it yet."

"Yeah. Nothing like commerce to get in the way of creativity." I flip through the printout of email addresses.

"Those are the most active 2,500 accounts. The website's database has a little over a hundred thousand registered users. If you need it all, I'll send you the file electronically."

Good grief, I hope this isn't going to require me investigating a hundred thousand people. Cripes. "Hopefully, I won't need it. So, tell me about the last contact you had with your mother. Did she act odd in any way?"

"Nope. She sent me a text to say she was going to Dunkin' for her morning usual."

Dunkin'? Oh, right. They dropped the 'donuts' from the name to sound healthier. Not sure what's sadder, that they'd try it or the people who fall for it. "Okay."

"That's it. Never heard from her again. The police found her car there and the security video showed a couple guys in a black van take her like chauffeurs. Mom didn't put up any fight according to them. They said she acted as if she expected them to be there."

I nod, think a moment, then make eye contact. "What makes you believe she didn't?"

"Umm. I just do. I know it's basic, but Mom just wouldn't get in a car with complete strangers. It's out of character. Yes, her going to Dunkin' was a daily routine. It's not like she randomly went there to meet these guys and stage a disappearance. Someone who'd been observing her would know she went to the place like clockwork. Mom always says a writer is a machine that converts coffee into alternate realities."

I chuckle. Well, this isn't the least amount I've ever had to work with on a case.

Scanning her thoughts, it's obvious Greta feels like none of this makes sense. At present, she's subconsciously thinking about the various times her mom decided to go wandering off randomly, and not one of them involved having people come get her. As in, she never took a shuttle to the airport. Whenever Zandra got it in her to pop off somewhere, she always drove herself to the airport. She also didn't ignore text messages and calls, making no effort to hide taking a trip on a sudden whim.

Her memory of the police is slightly different than what she described to me earlier. Initially, they did kind of come off like they figured the woman would return on her own, until Greta mentioned her mother never failed to respond to texts or calls previously. I'm starting to think someone possibly abducted her for ransom, taking advantage of Zandra's scatterbrained nature to trick her into believing she needed to go with them.

"Umm... so can you help?" asks Greta. She's probably wondering why I've been sitting here silent for a few minutes.

"Yes. I'll definitely help you find your mother." I offer a hand to shake.

She squeezes my fingers, desperation clear in the tightness of her grip. "Do you think I'm overreacting hiring you while the police are still looking?"

"Nah. We can never do too much to help the

ones we love."

Greta exhales, not quite relieved, but calmer than before. "What now?"

"I'll need as much info as you have. What's her address? Where's the Dunkin' she went to? Your contact information…"

"All right."

We spend a while talking, mostly her feeding me information I jot down on the back of the email address printout. No one has yet made any ransom demands, nor has she had any luck using the app to find her mother's cell phone. Sounds to me like someone turned it off. Suppose it's possible Zandra forgot to charge it and the battery died—but from what I've seen in Greta's memory, her mother isn't *that* absentminded. Her eccentricity mostly sounds like the sorts of things fringe movie producers do, like taking a trip to Costa Rica at the drop of a hat to research a story idea. We're not talking about someone who has a temporal fugue and winds up across the country living under an assumed name with no memory of their former life, just a whimsically nutty screenwriter who adores cheesy B-movies.

And she's apparently been abducted by two guys with a van.

Damn. This is the kind of case—especially

with security video showing the woman willingly going with her abductors—most PIs would probably pass on. For no reason I can put my finger on, my instincts tell me to get involved.

They also think I should hurry.

Chapter Three
Trust

Once Greta leaves, I do the most reasonable thing an investigator can do: teleport.

Hey, time's of the essence here.

No, I don't pop out of the chair in the middle of Starbucks. Bathroom stalls make for perfect launch pads. Or in one case, a hiding place. I'm looking at you grate underneath the sink. (Again, long story.) Thanks to visiting with Allison and her little apartment in Beverly Hills, I know the city well enough.

I summon the single flame...

...and appear in Beverly Gardens Park. With the help of my phone, I make my way into The Flats to Zandra Adams' house.

What I'm about to do is technically illegal, but it's not like anyone will notice—or remember if they catch me. I'm on the honor system. While someone with my powers *could* totally abuse the hell out of them, I trust myself.

Nothing appears out of the ordinary at the house, no signs of a break-in or other damage. After scoping around the exterior, I peer in a back window and teleport inside. A few minutes of exploring brings me to a room she most likely uses as her writing den. The whole room is pervasively dark brown, due to stained natural wood walls and ceiling. A couple of reading chairs, a cozy, old desk and even a fireplace add to the coziness. I gently look over papers and such, in case she might have left notes or something potentially helpful in terms of finding her. Sadly, the only paperwork out on the desk are sixteen pieces of fan mail she'd been in the midst of reading.

On the off chance a disappointed or overly intense fan is responsible, I skim the letters. None seem like the product of a disturbed mind except for one guy who thought *Vampire Fiona* should've been an Oscar contender. Yeah, umm, no. Not even if taken as a comedy. I can see it fitting a niche: movies so bad they're good. People who adore cheesy camp like it.

Speaking as a former blood-sucking vampire, people *don't* spew geysers of blood when bitten, stabbed, or decapitated. Sure, some arterial spurting will occur in cases of sudden decapitation, but it's a pulsing spurt only as wide as the carotid artery—not a continuous 500-gallon firehose blast that sprays blood all over the ceiling. They must have had a tanker truck of artificial blood on the set while filming.

Anyway, I spend a little over an hour exploring the house before concluding there is nothing here of any use to my investigation into where Zandra Adams went. So… I teleport out and make my way to the Dunkin' one-point-eight miles away. The manager initially doesn't want to let me see the video, but after a little mental convincing, brings me into the back office.

The security video feed is handily available as a separate file on the office computer because he'd already copied an excerpt of the feed for the cops. A camera in the front window monitoring the parking lot records a full-size black passenger van with no markings rolling to a stop. Two men get out, one pale and muscular, the other dark brown, sinewy, and Middle Eastern looking. He's got a funky aura on the video, a thin layer of pale, glowing energy surrounding his body. Both men stand by the van in the manner of patient chauffeurs awaiting their client.

Zandra walks into view fifty-eight seconds into the clip, exiting the Dunkin'. The woman looks like a fortune-teller in a long, hippie-style tie dye skirt, sandals, and a hideous orange-red-and-yellow sweater. Both men approach her, the Middle-Eastern guy offering a wide smile as he extends his hand to her. She pauses, cocking her head in a 'who the heck are these guys' manner, but the skepticism lasts only seconds before she smiles back at him.

The video has no sound, and my lip-reading skills are iffy at best. As far as I can tell, the man says something like 'we're here to give you a ride to the meeting.' Zandra's body language gives off a sense of someone who'd just been reminded about something they'd completely forgotten about. She follows them to the van and gets in, acting as if she wants to.

Only... I know better.

Her gait changed. Zandra Adams is not a heavyset woman, though she's not exactly skinny. Most of her weight is below the waist, so to speak. Combined with her flighty personality, she had a bit of a whimsical waddle to her step before. I could practically hear her muttering to herself like an anthropomorphic rabbit worrying about being late. However, on the short walk across the parking lot to the van, she plodded in a graceless stride devoid of any personality.

I know the stride.

I've inflicted it on people.

It's the same way a person moves when they're under mind control. Minimal personality. A robot set to task.

Shit.

The angle of the camera doesn't offer a great view of the van, but there is a second-and-a-half as it turns to leave where the rear license plate is sorta visible. Places like this are cheap with their surveillance equipment. The camera isn't the best. Distance and a crummy camera make the plate mostly a blur. My eyes are quite a bit sharper than a mortal's, however. Alas, my vision still isn't enough to get a full plate, only the first four digits: 7—either 8 or B—GX.

I thank the manager, head outside to the trash area where no one is watching, and teleport straight home to my office. Grumbling, I flop in my chair and pick up the phone.

Need a friend with access to the motor vehicle systems. I call Detective Sherbet. It hasn't been too long since we spoke, maybe two weeks before my European vacation from hell. He'd been working on a nasty home invasion case. Man dead, wife in critical condition, two kids missing. They had a suspect in for interrogation, but the guy wouldn't crack. Sherbet had a real strong hunch the dude was involved, so he asked me to cheat by reading his mind. Turns out, the dead man's ex-wife hired him to kill the guy. The kids saw the suspect shoot their stepfather. Lacking the nerve to kill children, he'd abducted them to buy himself time. He had them locked in his basement. The cops picked him up before he had a chance to make up his mind between killing them or fleeing to Mexico. I compelled the guy to confess.

Not exactly ethical, but it's not like I forced him to lie. More like forced him *not* to lie.

"Sherbet," says the detective by way of answering.

"Hey, it's me. How goes?"

"Ehh. It goes." His chair springs creak. "Could be better, could be worse."

"That good, huh?"

"Having some difficulty talking to the boy," says Sherbet.

Ahh. Now I understand his mood. His son, Zayn, is by all outward appearances, gay. Detective Sherbet isn't exactly thrilled about it, but he also loves his son. The problem is, the man's so old school he has no idea how to even talk about such things. Big strong silent cop type, right? Doesn't do the soft and sensitive thing very well at all.

"How is he?" I ask.

"Okay. He's been sneaking around. God, I hope he's not getting drunk or high."

"He's probably got a boyfriend and he's afraid about how you'll react. Doesn't seem the type to be into drugs."

Sherbet chuckles. "Yeah, he doesn't. Guess that's why I'm on edge. Not sure how to handle it."

"The same way any parent handles their kid dating. Be supportive and happy for him, and make sure the boyfriend isn't a creep or mistreating him."

"Right…" The cringe comes over the phone so thick it's tangible. "Easier said than done."

"Do what I did when I walked into Tammy's room and found a boy there."

He whistles. "Whoa! You did not catch her in bed with a boy under your roof."

My turn to laugh. "I didn't say they were in bed. Just in her room. He snuck in through the window."

"No shit? How long ago? You didn't mention this before."

"Because it was a non-issue. She was fifteen, the boy sixteen. Tammy only dated him twice. I think she was mad at me for something and snuck him in the house thinking it would start a fight. I walked in on them kissing."

"Wow. So what'd you do?"

"Aside from confronting the inevitability of my kid growing up, I told her sneaking behind my back was a no-go, but I'd rather she brought boys home than went somewhere she felt unsafe. Took the wind right out of her sails." Of course, Tammy knew how I really felt—contained panic—but mostly at the idea of her growing up. It totally caught her off guard to watch me set aside the reaction she'd expected because I wanted her to stay safe. No argument happened.

Luckily, she didn't really date much. A girl who knows exactly what's going on in a guy's mind isn't going to waste time on someone who's merely trying to get in her pants as fast as possible.

"Hmm." Spring creaks come over the phone.

I can picture him squirming in his chair at the idea of seeing his son kissing a boy. Honestly, I kinda squirmed the same way watching Tammy and that boy lock lips. She's my little girl, dammit. I hadn't been ready for her to become a teenager.

Deep breaths, Sam. She's not a child anymore.

"This a social call or you need a favor?" asks Sherbet.

He's clearly trying to change the subject. No point pushing him. "Both. The favor part's about a missing person case I just took on." I give him the details. "We're looking for a black Mercedes van, license plate starting with 78GX or 7BGX. Video quality was crap. The last two letters were a blur of pixels."

"I do not understand why people bother getting cameras if they're going to be cheap about it." Detective Sherbet sighs. "All right, give me a bit to look into this. I'll call ya back as soon as there's information to pass on."

"You are the best. Thank you."

He chuckles. "Thanks. And thanks again for the help with that Mendoza thing."

"Anytime. What happened? Are the kids okay?"

"Yeah. Rattled, but who can blame them. The mother's in physical therapy. Bullet didn't damage the spine too much. They think she'll be able to walk again."

I cringe, shaking my head. "That poor

woman."

"Take care, Sam."

"You, too. Don't become a cliché."

He laughs.

I've been teasing him lately about being the cop who's close to retirement, and something crazy happens on his last case. Sherbet's only in his later fifties, so he's not exactly aging out of the force anytime soon. It's purely me yanking his chain about getting older.

After we hang up, I sit there trying to think about my next step. This case has already gotten into strange territory. Someone with powers of mind control abducted Zandra Adams? May or may not be a vampire. The broad daylight abduction is a mark in the 'not vampires' column. However, as I proved multiple times in varying degrees of discomfort, it's not completely impossible for a vampire to tolerate sun with precautions and or magic. Maybe a real vampire—other than me—saw the movies she made and wanted to have a word about the quality. Or lack thereof.

Nah. Wouldn't be worth the effort.

The woman didn't have tons of money or power in Hollywood. No ransom demands or any contact from the kidnappers have surfaced. Maybe this vampire is one of her rabid fans who desired to meet her in person? Ack. I hope he's not intending to *turn* her into a vampire.

Hang on. I shouldn't get ahead of myself here. This man might not be a vampire at all, but something else. I've never seen an aura like his before, like the corona of the sun around him, only pale rather than orangey, and thin. The instant Tammy sees this guy in my head, she's going to make a joke about vampires who sparkle in movies. This dude didn't look the same, though, more like a human eclipsing a ghostly copy of himself, only a little bit of the ghost's glow visible around the edges.

Tammy goes by down the hall without stopping to say anything to me. Wow, it's later than I thought. She must've gotten back from school while I'd been watching video in the Dunkin' manager's office.

I move around the desk and jog over to the doorway, and stick my head in the hallway. "Hey, Tam. What's up?"

"Nothing," she slows, but doesn't stop.

"Where are you going?"

"Out."

"Out?" I ask.

"Yes, Mom. Out. Why do you always have to be up my butt about where I'm going?"

"I assure you, I am not up your butt."

"Feels like it."

"First, gross. And I'm sorry. I can't stop myself from being worried about our crazy existence. Any moment could be the last ones we have together. My greatest fear is losing you and Anthony. Like my greatest fear ever."

Of course, my second greatest fear is losing her after we've had an argument and the last words I'll ever say to her came out heated.

She sighs. "Dammit, Mom. Thanks for making me feel guilty."

"Not *trying* to make you feel guilty."

"Yeah." She hangs her head. "You know, you make it really dang hard to be a surly teenager."

I walk down the hall to where she's hovering by the archway to the living room. "Except surly teenagers don't say 'surly.'"

"Well, I do."

"Well, better live it up while you can, kiddo. You're only going to be a teen for two more years. Crap."

"What?"

"I'm old."

Tammy laughs, teetering back into the wall. "Mom, you're not *that* old. You're not even thirty yet. Why, you don't look a day over twenty-seven."

Eye roll time.

"Seriously, Mom. Lots of women celebrate the anniversary of their twenty-first birthday over and over again. With you, it's actually kinda literal."

"That would mean I'm on the... twenty-fourth anniversary of my twenty-first."

"If you say so. Not a fan of math."

"Even basic math?"

"Any math."

"Well, are you ready for things to get really weird?"

She huffs. "It's already weird."

"No, I mean are you ready for people to think of us as sisters? You're the kid sister now. Eventually, people seeing us together will think you're the older sister... then someday, you're going to be mistaken for *my* mother."

"Ugh." She shivers and holds her arm out. "Do it now. Just bite me and turn me."

The only reason I don't completely freak is she's done this before and it's obviously a joke. I pretend bite her on the wrist. She falls into me, pantomime dying. We end up laughing for a little while before she resumes drifting toward the door.

"So... where are you going?"

"Just out with my friends. Not really sure

what we'll be doing yet." She flaps her arms in kind of a shrug.

"All right. If you're going out to do something you don't want to tell me you're going to be doing, at least be careful and don't overindulge. If things get out of hand *please* call me for a ride. I promise I won't make a big deal out of it. Much rather have you home safe than get in a car with someone who's been drinking."

She blushes—her usual response to being busted, but nods. "Okay, Ma."

I take a few steps to close distance and squeeze her hand. "Sure, I'd rather you stay completely sober, but I'm not a hypocrite. You're way tamer than me at your age. If you need to call me for your safety, you have my word I'll pretend not to have seen anything I should yell at you for."

"I said okay. Sheesh."

Of course, she's eighteen now and we're no longer poor. Maybe she should have a car of her own.

Tammy squeaks, eyes widening in a 'holy shit, really?!' expression.

"We'll talk about it. The Momvan can't take much more of you driving her." I'd been considering giving her the van, but it's been deteriorating faster than expected.

My daughter releases the bastard offspring of a snort-giggle-laugh. "She can't tolerate much more of *anyone* driving her."

"Yeah, yeah… Maybe we'll get matching pink Priuses."

She cringes. "I know you're kidding. At least make it black ones."

A tiny *beep* from outside makes her spin toward the door. "Veronica's here. Gotta go."

"Okay. Have a good time. And try not to overdo it."

"Wow." Tammy blinks. "So weird not hearing you say not to drink."

"You already know how I feel. Didn't seem productive to repeat it over and over again. It'll only make you resent hearing it. And"—I sigh—"you are eighteen now. I need to trust you."

"That can't be easy for you."

"Trusting you isn't the hard part."

She strolls back over to me for a quick hug. "I know. You still think of me as a five-year-old."

"You'll always be my little Tam Tam," I say. "Even when you're a little old lady."

Tammy sticks out her tongue. "I'm gonna be a badass little old lady."

"Let's just make sure you get there."

"Any reason why Elizabeth just popped into your thoughts, Ma?"

"Damn if I know."

"I, um, might have forgotten to tell you something."

"Uh oh."

She bites her lip. "Yesterday, at school, I got like this weird feeling in second period."

"Weird how?"

Tammy stares intently into my eyes. In seconds, a sense of ominous dread falls over me. The only way I can really think to describe it is feeling like I'm standing out in a field somewhere in Oklahoma in the moment before a giant tornado manifests. Powerful energy—somewhere—is nearby and it's not in a good mood.

She relaxes and the sense fades.

"What the heck?"

"You know how I can talk in your head? I've figured out how to send feelings the same way. Couldn't think how to describe it. What you just felt is how I felt for a while yesterday for no reason."

"Ominous dread?"

"Maybe. Except it didn't feel like something was coming for me specifically. Just powerful stuff close by. It only lasted a few minutes."

"Hmm."

Beep, beep.

"Later, Mom." She waves and runs out to Veronica's car, an older blue Malibu.

Not a good sign. No, not her getting in the car. I mean her feeling a weird sense of power right about the time Zandra Adams met the Middle Eastern possible vampire with a wonky aura. If Tammy felt him all the way from Fullerton... this guy is going to be a big problem.

Of course, me being me, I'm more worried about the party she's going to.

Chapter Four
A Bit Different

Know what sucks more than Mondays? Tuesdays.

It's not so much the day itself or its position in the week. It's more me having poured an entire day into the search for Zandra Adams and being no closer to figuring out what happened. I even called Kingsley, Fang, and Max the alchemist to ask them if either recognized the weird aura the one guy had. My opinion about the dude being a vampire is still merely a theory based on his apparent use of mind control. Of course, we're not the only creatures out there who can do it.

None of the guys have ever heard of an aura

like that, especially one visible to cameras. Fang commented it can't be a 'traditional' aura, or what most people mean when they say 'aura.' It's some kind of energy radiating from the guy… but what it means eludes us. Max sounded concerned when I mentioned it, but didn't say anything. He probably suspects something but doesn't trust his theory enough to scare me with it yet.

It's unlikely the dude was a merman. According to Kingsley, someone under the compulsion of a mer-person's charm acts all sorts of lovestruck. Zandra didn't. At me describing the man as Middle Eastern, Max floated the idea of him possibly being a Rakshasa using an illusion spell to appear human. Usually, they have the heads of tigers. One problem with his theory: no one has seen or heard of a Rakshasa since the early 1800s, and the last sighting occurred in India. It's possible there are too few people who believe in them for any to remain around. Or maybe whatever 'spin the wheel and see where it lands' process responsible for determining what a dark master turns into hasn't come up on 'Rakshasa' in a while. Allison thinks an illusion spell *might* be responsible for the weird glowing light on the camera. We tested using her magic, but any illusions she made appeared ordinary in pictures. Frustratingly, it didn't prove Rakshasa out. They might have an entirely different type of magic from Allie.

Either way, a megalomaniacal cat-humanoid doesn't seem at all likely to abduct a B-list movie director. For that matter, neither does any supernatural creature, really. Silly as it sounds, my theory about this guy being a real vampire who happened to be a fan of her movies remains the most likely explanation in my head.

Sad, right? Considering how unlikely it is.

I'm presently sitting behind my desk in my office feeling grateful my supernatural powers do not include laser eye beams. The frustrated glare I've been aiming at my wall would have burned down the house if I had such a power. For most of the morning, I interviewed employees and even a few regulars at the Dunkin' where Zandra disappeared. Not one person remembered her—including the manager who showed the video to the cops, and me.

Something supernatural is *definitely* involved here. Worse, whatever erased their memories did so in a way where I couldn't dig anything back up. Normal vampire memory tinkering, as I understand it, is something like the way computers store files on a hard drive. Haven't thought about this tech stuff since my

HUD days, but it's an apropos analogy. A memory is like a file on a disk. When a person goes to think about the memory, their brain looks at a particular file. Vampires create new files and implant a 'pointer' that refers to the false memory. On a computer, if someone deletes a file, the system doesn't actually destroy the original file—it merely edits a directory table to consider the disk space the file occupies as being empty. Until something overwrites the space, the file is still technically there. Our—well, the FBI's—lab could usually recover any data even if someone deleted it.

Anyway, the point of this is… whatever happened to the Dunkin manager and the employees was comparable to the file being utterly destroyed. Sometimes, vampiric memory tinkering can come undone and the person regains access to the real memory. In this case, the people's real memories of Zandra's visit that day are just plain gone.

I can think of three possible explanations for this. One—and highly unlikely—a being along the scope of the Devil did it. Basically, a demigod. Two: an old-as-hell vampire might be able to do it, especially if they're connected to Elizabeth somehow since her telepathic powers are off the charts. The third possibility, and it's a total guess on my part, is magic.

What's killing me here is, nothing I've been able to find about Zandra's life or accomplishments warrants the attention of anything or anyone powerful enough to do this. That is, unless Dracula got extremely pissed off about her ridiculous portrayal of vampires. Again, seems kinda doubtful. Most actual vampires love crappy vampire movies because it distorts the truth and makes them more of a myth. Way easier to hide if fewer people take their existence seriously.

No employee remembered seeing her that day. I also interviewed fourteen other people, all of whom worked with her in one capacity or another within the past two years or had regular contact with her (like neighbors). Every one of them gave me a different, but plausible, story for why Zandra wasn't around. Usually, it involved going on vacation or traveling for a movie shoot, or going out of state to visit family somewhere. Everyone had a different story, and all of them had memories of her giving them that explanation.

Another thing about vampires playing with memories: inserting a new false memory of something that never happened is perhaps the easiest thing to do. It has no reality to conflict with, so there's much less chance of it slipping loose by itself or even triggering doubts in the mind of the victim. For example, I could make someone think they saw a fleeting glimpse of a celebrity and they'd go to their grave swearing they'd met Madonna. The less impactful to their life, the easier it is to convince them. Adding a memory of a false childhood pet would be more difficult to make stick since the person would constantly remember events or stuff and *not* how the pet had been part of it. But inserting a twenty-second conversation with a neighbor saying they're going to London for a month? Yeah, as good as reality.

It's almost one in the afternoon and I'm so frustrated my computer monitor is quaking in fear because I'm *that* close to throwing it across the room. It's been a while since frustration and excess energy have built up to the point sitting still is impossible. Gotta do something to Zen out enough to think. Hmm.

Yanno... Anthony was pretty worried about Jacky.

Weird for me to randomly think of him, but I used to be in the habit of going there to blow off excess energy. Why not now? I've run out of possible ways to investigate Zandra's disappearance without involving witchcraft, magic, or alchemy—and believe me, all three are on my to-do list.

I change into a T-shirt and sweat pants—over shorts in case the gym is hot—then head outside and hop in the Momvan. The door emits a serious creak when it closes, though it doesn't look damaged. Except for a mild bit of denting on the hood from where Mindy Hogan's face bounced off it, the old girl's in decent shape considering everything I've put her through. It's so stupid of me to get sentimental over a car. Ya know what? I think she'll stay. Even if I get something newer to drive, gonna keep the Momvan because she's part of the family.

At least, until she legit falls to pieces or road cars no longer exist.

How scary is that thought? I might be around to see flying cars or the end of gasoline engines.

Whatever. Too far in the future to worry about now.

***

Downtown Fullerton is trying oh so hard to be hip.

People the age I appear to be are supposed to call it 'gentrified.' Well-off hipsters think things are 'in step.' People my actual age grumble about how expensive everything down here is getting. Everything has a modern vibe or an 'old-looking but new' grunge aesthetic—except Jacky's Gym. The place hasn't changed much at all appearance-wise since he first opened it in like 1974 or so.

The town council had been giving him grief over being an 'eyesore' until I helped out a little. For some strange reason, whenever local businesses complain about the place, a veritable army of inspectors and code enforcement agents swarm their shop instead. Strange, right? So, yeah, the merchants in the area have all decided to leave Jacky's place alone. And seriously, the gym doesn't look bad. It's merely normal. You'd think the hipster crowd would find it appealing since it's basically a time machine back to the 1970s.

Parking's a bitch, though. I totally should've flown or teleported. Oh well. So I have a two-block walk.

I don't think Jacky has seen me since my experience with the Red Rider. Last time here, my skin didn't have any real color to it other than what makeup I added. He knows I'm a little different than normal people—as in, supernaturally strong—but I've never told him the exact truth.

Honestly, the man doesn't need more mental burdens. Losing his wife last year hit him hard enough.

Jacky's standing in the rear left corner of the gym. Beside him, a heavy bag sits on the floor. He's got his fists against his hips, socket wrench in one hand, glaring at the chain hanging from the ceiling. Looks like he ordered a new one to replace the busted one Anthony threw out for him. No one else is in the place. The two boxing rings that take up most of the right side are empty, as are the workout machines and free weights.

"Hey, Jacky," I say, wandering over to him. "Need a hand?"

He looks over at me. For a few seconds, his face shows zero sign of recognition and even a trace of suspicion, like 'is this skinny broad really offering to lift a heavy bag?' To him, I'm skinny since I don't have the muscles of a professional female boxer. Okay, maybe my body is on the thinner side of average, but I'm no runway model. Even before becoming a vampire, I had enough arm strength to make it through training. Not that HUD agents had to do tons of hand-to-hand drills, but we had some.

"Jacky?" I ask. "It's me, Sam."

"Oh." He blinks, waves dismissively, then

rubs his forehead. "Of course ya are. Got too damn frustrated with this bag to think straight."

"Wow, it got here pretty fast. Ant told me about the broken one."

"Yeah. Darn thing finally gave out. You Moons are hard on my equipment. Ordered this one a couple days ago, before even takin' the old one down. Almost got the bastard up a couple times but my damn back isn't wanting to cooperate."

"Come on, Jacky, you're getting a bit old to lift stuff like this."

He grumbles. "I'm seventy-seven. I'm not useless."

"Didn't say you're useless. But you should have someone younger lift a hundred-pound bag for you. Besides, how are you supposed to hold it up and tighten the bolt at the same time?" I grab the thing and hoist it up. To me, its weight is barely noticeable.

"Showin' off again, eh, lass?" He chuckles, though it sounds kinda angry. Still, he reaches up to secure the bolt. After Anthony launched a heavy bag halfway across the gym a year or so ago, Jacky decided to bolt them to the hangers rather than leaving them merely on hooks. The socket ratchets a few times, then he steps back to look it over. "All done. Why not give it a couple shots, warm it up?"

"Heh. Okay. I need to blow off a little steam anyway."

I spend a few minutes punching the bag, weaving around as if boxing. Though my frustration at the case is high, my control is higher. Lately, I've been sparring with an older vampire named Sebastian, brushing up on sword techniques. Punching a static heavy bag is boring and easy by comparison. I do not wallop the bag hard enough to tear the chain off the ceiling. Jacky, arms folded like the old coach he is, watches me, making faces at my form and technique.

"You should wear gloves, lass. Your knuckles will split."

I look down... and he's right. Middle knuckle on my right hand is already splitting... and already healing too. So, I let the ex-boxer strap some gloves on me, then resume the onslaught.

If only the old guy knew I'd killed one iteration of the literal Devil and also flung myself down the throat of a dragon the size of a commercial jetliner, maybe he wouldn't be so critical of my boxing stance. Then again, this *is* Jacky. Of course he would be.

While I'm test-punching the bag, we chat

randomly about life, mostly catching up. He needles me a bit in regard to prodding Anthony to reconsider his decision not to try going into the professional boxing circuit. The gentle nagging proves Anthony hasn't told him anything about the supernatural stuff affecting him. A lesser person would have totally made themselves rich and famous. Pride at the sort of man he's becoming makes me tear up a little. If he was here now and not in school, I'd totally have hugged him.

And he'd totally have complained about it.

"Wow, Sam. You look amazing. Your form, not so much."

I smirk. "Thanks. And you're in decent shape yourself for an old man."

"Oh, them's fightin' words, lass," he says with a wink.

"Hah."

"Still working out?" He starts to give a disdainful glance at the bag, so I hammer it a little harder than humanly possible. "Ahh... seems ya are."

I catch the bag to stop it from swaying, glancing at him in concern. Not sure if he's teasing me or genuinely forgot about my enhanced strength. "Yeah, though my workouts have gotten a bit extreme lately."

"Ach. Tell me yer not caught up in the cross-fit nonsense?"

"No, nothing *that* crazy. Been training with a sword."

"Sword, ya say?"

"Yup."

Jacky nods like I'd said something completely normal. "Long as ya keep up with it, should keep ya fighting trim."

"How are you holding up?" I ask.

He opens his mouth to answer, then seems to remember Mary's gone and his expression falls. I get the feeling he misses her in ways no words could adequately describe. The man's not okay, but he'd never admit it, tough guy and all.

A faint bluish glimmer drifts out from the hallway leading to the back section containing the office, storage area, and locker rooms-slash-showers. I glance at the apparition, which lingers for a moment or two before disappearing. Hmm. A ghost. Never saw one in here before. I've seen an angel in here. And Dracula. But not a ghost.

Wonder if it's Mary waiting for him? Huh, I wonder how it works to be with someone after death. From what I understand, there is an incredible afterlife. Something darn close to heaven—as in beauty, peace, love and flying. I also know that our stay in the afterlife is only temporary. After all, reincarnation beckons. Basically, the afterlife is a stopover on the way to rebirth. No one's really ever mentioned how many lives my soul has gone through. Could be hundreds of years between each one where I'd been somewhere else. Maybe 'heaven' is something like what happened when I incarnated as a dragon in Talos' realm. Souls incarnate for a while in some other dimension, then come back. Or maybe heaven—eternal heaven—is the eventual end result of multiple reincarnations after a particular soul has learned everything it needs to.

Who knows… but she does seem to be waiting for him.

"Get them hands up, kid," says Jacky, dropping into a boxing stance.

He's too old to spar with, but I humor him a little, barely defending or dodging his playful jabs. He's not really trying to spar, more like shadow-box, testing my defenses. Damn, he looks frail. In-between limp punches, he asks me about how the kids are doing, and we end up talking about how fast life goes by.

"Ya look great for forty-five, kid." He tries to bop me in the nose, but I duck easily.

"Must be the healthy vegan lifestyle."

He chuckles, jabbing rapidly a few times. Whoa, flashes of his previous greatness—nice. "Bah. Kids these days. They're gonna turn into avocados. You gotta eat more than veggies to live. An' how the heck do they toast them?"

I chuckle. "They don't toast the avocado. They put it on actual toast. Never tried it though. I'm kinda hooked on psychic energy now. Low fat and sugar free." I duck a haymaker.

"Psychic energy? That some new kinda shake?" He swings faster, adding more power. "Wow, kid. You're fast. Really got something, there. Ever think about going pro?"

Damn, he's not teasing. He totally knows I can't go pro because of supernatural reasons. Sure, he's taken more than his share of head shots in his younger days, but he's totally off balance now. Both mentally and physically.

"Maybe we should slow it down a bit, Jacky," I say, weaving.

"Nonsense. We just got started." He tries to knock my jaw off.

I block as gently as possible, trying to hold onto his arm to get him to stop.

"Good. Good. Hands up." He attempts to maneuver to my left, nearly tripping over his own feet.

"Jacky, hang on... something's not right." I grab his shoulder with one gloved hand, arm in the other, holding him steady. "Are you feeling okay?"

"Bah. You know damn well I haven't felt okay since Mary..." He clenches his jaw, unable to say the word 'died.' A bead of sweat trickles down his reddened face.

The ghostly spot reappears closer to us, getting brighter. I get the sense it's not a threatening brightness, more anticipatory. She knows something's wrong, too. Uh, oh.

"Oh," says Jacky. "You told me, didn't you? Can't go pro. Some crazy *X-Files* type stuff."

"Something like that, yeah. I'm a little closer to human now. C'mon, why don't you sit down and relax?"

"Sorry." He gives up on shadow boxing, rubbing his face. "Didn't keep my hands up as much as I should have. The old brain's been bounced around too much. Losing things here and there."

"It happens when people get a little older." I gently guide him toward the front desk where he can sit. "You shouldn't be sparring after, you know, hanging heavy bags."

"You're probably right, but I—" He cringes and grabs his left arm. His face gets even redder. Speechless, he looks up at me with a 'what's going on?' expression.

His thoughts contain a stabbing pain like someone fired an arrow through his left arm into his chest. Shit!

He's having a heart attack.

"Hang on, Jacky!" I grab him and teleport us both to St. Jude Medical Center, aiming for the ambulance entrance.

Of the handful of people standing around, no one seems to notice us come out of nowhere. One good thing about smartphones: they make teleporting easy. Fewer memories to tinker with since everyone's always absorbed with tiny screens and not looking at the world. Jacky slumps unconscious in my arms. I carry him inside.

"Hey!" I shout. "Need a doctor here. He's in the middle of a heart attack."

Someone in a white coat runs over, looks him over quickly, and shouts down the hall for a gurney while 'helping' me carry Jacky in that direction. A swarm of nurses and a cop appear almost out of thin air and help relocate him to an ER bed while another woman gently pulls me back.

I don't bother fighting her, standing there watching them push Jacky away.

"Are you his granddaughter?" asks the woman with her hand on my arm.

Once Jacky's out of sight, I peer down at her dark brown hand. Even though I don't know this woman at all, her touch is comforting. None of the hospital staff knows what I saw in Jacky's head. He wasn't suicidal, but he wanted Death to hurry up and find him. Old Irish Catholics don't do the suicide thing, after all.

"Ma'am?" asks the woman.

I'm not sure if she's a nurse, an administrative clerk, or a nurse promoted to management. She's not scrambling off with the care team, so she must be option two or three.

"Umm, no," I say. "Family friend. Jacky doesn't have any living relatives as far as I know."

"All right." She nods once. "How'd you find him?"

"He owns a gym on North Harbor Boulevard. Started going there years ago. We became friends. Jacky's wife died last year. He didn't take it too well. Today, I went there to check up on him and found him trying to lift a heavy bag." I explain him getting worked up, then starting to have a heart attack. "I got him here as fast as I could."

"Mind helping me out with whatever information you have?"

"Sure."

The woman introduces herself as Paula. I follow her to a small office and answer as many questions as I can about Jacky. He never mentioned having any family other than his wife, and I'm clueless about his medical history other than his being a retired boxer. As long as I'd known him, he'd been healthy as an ox.

"No next of kin?" asks Paula.

"None that he's ever mentioned. I can try to look into it." I show her my private investigator ID. "You can put me down as the contact person for now."

Any hesitation Paula has at putting a non-relative down as the primary contact disintegrates under a brief mental prod.

"You'll let me know as soon as I can see him?" I ask.

"Someone will, yes. Please have a seat in the waiting area." Paula offers a sympathetic smile.

"All right. Thanks. I really should go lock the doors to his place. I'll be back as soon as possible."

She nods, already entering Jacky's info in the computer.

I hurry to the nearest bathroom—and teleport back to the gym.

Chapter Five
Grandpa

By some miracle, the place doesn't appear to have been robbed.

Okay, maybe I'm emotional. Downtown isn't too bad really... and it's incredibly strange being in the gym when it's library quiet. Usually it's full of sweating women, multiple TVs on, lots of trainers shouting, weights clanking... Sure, it's a weekday and a little early for anyone to show up yet, but it's never been this quiet when I've come before.

I stand there daydreaming about when I first met Jacky, my first time deciding to give boxing lessons a try. Damn, did I sweat like hell. I remember him saying something about me 'sweating like a man,' and he liked it. Sounds creepy as hell to have a man say he loves my sweat, but his words and his meaning hadn't quite been on the same page. Wasn't anything pervy. He didn't have a sweat fetish or anything. It had been Jacky's way of saying he liked that I put in enough effort to work up a real sweat.

Never did bother wondering how an undead vampire *could* sweat, but whatever. Probably part of the whole 'pretending to be human' thing. The new me still sweats. My heart's also beating for real now, and I have a body temperature. No one's done any testing on me, but my suspicion is I've become something closer to Anthony. He's immortal but not undead. Truth is, I worry if a bullet to the heart is a problem for me now.

My instinct says probably not. As a 'traditional' vampire before, catching a bullet in the old blood pump ended up being less annoying than indigestion after an iffy Taco Bell run. I'm fairly certain it won't kill me as a psychic vampire either, but it might momentarily incapacitate me more than it once did. And no, I do not have any rush to test.

Once the nostalgia wears off, I run to the back room and check the other exit by the dumpsters to make sure it's locked. That done, I head to the counter and grab a piece of paper, making a note for the front door:

Jacky's Gym temporarily closed due to medical emergency.

I write my official PI phone number under it and add 'for inquiries or concerns' next to it.

After taping the sign to the glass door, I lock it and head into the back office. A few minutes of searching leads me to a book with important contact information. Jacky is old school and doesn't believe in computers, thankfully. He's got an entry for a lawyer, Gloria Levine. I add her number to my contacts. Maybe it's morbid of me, but my gut feeling here is Jacky's going to throw this fight. He wants nothing more than to be with his wife Mary again. The ghost I'm sure came to visit *had* to be her. She brightened when he started feeling pain. Since no malice radiated from the spirit, she must've been sensing his proximity to death.

Damn. I sigh. Anthony is going to be upset. He's going to be *more* upset if he doesn't have any chance to say goodbye to a man who'd basically become his grandfather. Once again, I check both doors to make sure they're locked, shut off all the lights, then teleport back to the Momvan and drive to Sunny Hills High, where both my kids are at the moment.

The school day isn't quite over, but they're in last period. Still, minutes could be the difference between saying goodbye and not getting the chance. I tell the school his step-grandfather is in critical condition after suffering a heart attack and they let me pull him from class. One of the office women calls the room he's in, telling the teacher to send Anthony to the office.

My son appears in a few minutes, walking lazily down the hall with a confused expression.

He spots me waiting by the door, becomes concerned, and jogs up to me. "Ma, what's up?"

"It's Jacky," I say, a little over a whisper. "He's had a heart attack."

My son's face loses most of its color—and all of the nonchalance. "What happened?"

"I'll tell you on the ride."

He nods once, then hurries after me to the Momvan.

On the way to St. Jude, I explain everything, including me seeing a ghostly presence. Considering the amount of time my son spent at the gym the past few years, he has to know Jacky well enough to realize he wants to be with his wife. That doesn't stop him from getting emotional and asking why this happened over and over.

"Why did he have to be stupid and try to hang the heavy bag himself? I told him I'd do it for him."

"Some people have a hard time accepting growing old. It's difficult for them to ask for help doing things they could once do easily on their own."

"He's too stubborn to die," grumbles Anthony. "Why do you think he's going to?"

I squeeze the steering wheel. "Not saying it's what I want to happen. He's seriously depressed. You know that. Men like him don't accept 'depression' as a real thing or deal with showing any kind of weakness. I think he wants to be with Mary."

"But he's not even old yet!" Anthony starts to make a fist, but ends up grabbing his hair instead of punching the dashboard. "He's not old enough to die yet."

My son's not too big on crying. Even as a little boy, his reaction to things like skinned knees or hurting himself ended up being what I called 'dammit face.' From like eleven or so onward, he got quiet in moments of high emotion. The few times he's cried have all involved death or near-death like when Danny died, for example. Or when Talos fell out of the sky at Mindy Hogan's farm and they all thought me dead for what to them had been about fifteen minutes. Tammy quietly let me know Anthony had been crying... to prepare me, she said, in case he acted unusually clingy for a while.

His stoicism isn't too shocking. He had a brush with death at age seven, after all. Takes a lot to make my kid cry.

He's composed himself by the time we arrive at St. Jude. We take seats in the waiting area, and he doesn't shy away from me putting an arm around his shoulders.

A short while later, a nurse walks up to us. "Excuse me, are you Samantha?"

"Yes."

"About Mr. Jacky O'Brien?"

Anthony stands. "How is he?"

"Resting. The doctors have stabilized him. He's in an ICU ward. You can see him now if you like, but not for too long," says the nurse.

Both of us nod.

She leads us down a hall to an elevator, up one floor, down another hall, and into the ICU area.

As soon as we enter his room, I sense a presence in the back corner. The same blue glowing haze hangs there, giving off a sense of patiently waiting. Anthony either doesn't notice or chooses not to, rushing to Jacky's bedside and taking a knee.

In the short span of time from seeing him at the gym and now, he's practically withered away.

The figure in this hospital bed, hooked up to machines, IVs, and wires, looks like a fragile little old man closer to ninety than his seventy-seven years. Suppose it's a good sign they don't have a hose going down his throat. Even my oversensitive ears can't discern any signs of him struggling to breathe. The heart monitor emits a steady rhythmic beeping, a little slow, but not worrisomely so.

"Jacky…" Anthony gently squeezes his hand around the IV and finger monitor. "You're a fighter. You can beat this."

We listen to the steady beeping for a few minutes.

Anthony starts randomly talking about people from the gym, like a pair of old guys hanging out at a bar discussing up and coming fighters. My son chuckles while mentioning one guy who has a habit of guarding too high, making him easy to hit in the stomach, then cracks a joke about an older gentleman named Bill who shows up every day to lift free weights. Apparently, he can't figure out how to make the water cooler work, and they've been teasing him by claiming it's broken and the repair guy is 'coming soon' for weeks.

"C'mon, Jacky. Don't give up. People still need you," says Anthony, his voice at the verge of cracking. "*I* still need you."

My heart slides up into my throat. It's impossible for me to watch my son break down and not cry along with him. I walk up beside him and rest my hand on his shoulder.

"Thank you for being there for me. I'll never forget you, but you're not done yet." Anthony sniffles. "Who's gonna remind me to get my hands up?"

A faint smile appears on Jacky's lips.

"I-Is he gonna be okay?" whispers Anthony.

"I really don't know."

Anthony peers up at me. "You can't tell? Didn't you like, have a thing that lets you know?"

He's talking about the black aura I used to be able to see. In fact, I had seen it around him, at age seven, which is how I knew he was close to death.

"No. I don't drink blood anymore. Can't feel it when people are close to death." I fixate on Jacky's mental energy. "His mind is still strong."

Anthony takes that as reassurance.

Not sure if it is, to be honest. I now have the ability to sense the energy 'status' of a prospective meal. In the case of Jacky, his energy status barely registers on my radar. Knowing this allows me to avoid leaving someone a permanent vegetable. No, I can't kill people from 'drinking' too much of their energy. But... if I absorb every ounce of it, well, they end up in a situation worse than death. Their body is physically alive, but all the lights are off upstairs, so to speak. The only thing keeping it from being absolutely horrendous is the person doesn't exist in any way capable of being aware of suffering.

Speaking of which, it might mean total destruction of their soul/ghost.

Not completely sure there, but it's nothing I'd ever risk. Destroying a soul is way more evil than murdering a physical shell. Fortunately, I am quite capable of taking tiny bits of mental energy from individual people in a crowd. In the case of Jacky, his energy status barely registers on my radar. He's thoroughly exhausted.

Anthony talks to Jacky for another almost eight minutes about random stuff before the nurse returns.

"Mr. O'Brien needs to rest," she whispers.

"Okay." Anthony takes a few deep breaths to stop himself from crying. "Comin' back tomorrow, okay? Hospital says we have to leave now. The ref's counting, but you're gonna sit up before he gets to ten."

Jacky's still smiling slightly. No change. The heart monitor hasn't sped up or slowed since we walked in.

I glance toward the ghost in the corner. She —I assume—is giving off a sense of sadness, probably feeling bad for Anthony. Perhaps once we leave, she'll be able to speak to Jacky in his unconscious state somehow. Who knows?

"Thank you for being in Anthony's life." I rest my hand on Jacky's arm. "And thanks for teaching me a little of what you know. Hope you decide to stick around for a while, but I'll understand if you have places to go. I hear it's a wild ride. Stick close to her. You two might find each other again."

Anthony stands, rubbing his knee. "See ya tomorrow, Jacky."

"Night, 'old man,'" I say, smiling, hoping it annoys him enough to wake up so he can tell me off.

We walk out of the hospital under a heavy cloud of worry, not a word exchanged, even after we're both in the Momvan staring straight ahead. I can't even put the key in the ignition.

"He can't die," whispers Anthony. Seconds

later, he chuckles past tears. "So lame."

"Lame?"

"Dad... He just said, 'everything dies eventually. Except taxes.'"

"Mary was probably in the room with us," I say.

"Probably?" Anthony glances over at me. "You're not sure?"

"Not really. But a ghost was definitely there. Couldn't tell who. Just a cloud of blue light."

"Thought you could see ghosts."

"I can. If they try to hide from me, I see the blue light."

Anthony grabs a tissue from the cup holder and dabs his eyes. "Why would Mrs. O'Brien hide from us?"

"It's different for ghosts. She probably wanted to be alone with him." I rub Anthony's back. "He's a fighter."

"Yeah." My son leans against me, and surrenders to quiet sobs.

Chapter Six
Damn

As soon as we got home, Anthony went to his bedroom and logged into his video game.

Seemed odd to me at first, until I realized he wasn't really *playing* it as much as wanting to talk to his online friends. With the exception of Topher Grimes—I swear the kid has the perfect name for a private investigator or noir film character—and Dwayne Winston, two of his friends from school, the majority of his social attachments are people he's met in the game. His 'guild' friends as he calls them are almost a second family. He's telling them about Jacky, no doubt.

Like seven months ago, a girl in his guild a

little younger than him—I think she's fifteen—confided in him she was thinking of committing suicide because of bullying. Her parents stuck her with the name Lexus, and kids at school kept making jokes about 'riding' her. The nastier ones referred to her as an expensive ride. Anthony told me about it… so we went to Atlanta. Maybe I broke a few ethical boundaries by implanting mental commands in the kids teasing her to leave her alone, but the school administration wasn't doing anything about it.

It shouldn't surprise me how my son became so concerned and emotionally invested in the well-being of a girl all the way on the other side of the country he'd never met in person, never expected to meet in person, and only thought of as a friend—unlike another girl he's sweet on, Ainsley Cortez. Of course, Casanova hasn't said a word to her. I think he's afraid of inadvertently making her into a slave. Like me and Russel Baker, a mortal I tried dating before I realized why supernatural beings shouldn't become romantically involved with mortals.

It added a whole new wrinkle to when I had 'the talk' with my son. We still don't know one way or the other if whatever he's become will do the same thing. Until Danny decided to get involved, my son didn't have a resident dark master. Perhaps it's not so much being an immortal, but having one of them inside that causes mortals to become enthralled during a romantic relationship. Elves are, in some respects, supernatural and Kai hasn't turned my daughter into a mindless servant.

Speaking of my daughter, Tammy thinks Ant should ask Ainsley out since 'Mom can fix it if you mind control her.' Maybe…

So here I am, flopped on my sofa, staring at the ceiling. I wasn't ready for how hard it would hit me to see Jacky reduced from a vibrant guy to a fragile old man so rapidly. We'd been friends and maybe he'd kind of taken on something of a paternal role in my head. It's sad to say, but my actual father feels more like 'some guy who used to live in the same house as us.' My parents are almost certainly the reason I'm like I am with my kids, not wanting them to grow up. As disinterested as they'd been toward us, I'm going entirely in the other direction with Tammy and Anthony.

The idea of losing Jacky is hitting me like most people feel about losing their parents.

Again, sad to say, but when the day comes my actual parents leave the mortal realm for another spin on the Wheel of Reincarnation my reaction is most likely going to be about the same as how Tammy reacted to learning about Jacky: ugh, that sucks.

She's at Wendy's now, working.

I'm impressed, honestly. She could have quit and whined about us having all this money, so she didn't really need a part time job. Either she saw me thinking about how the point of teens working isn't the money but the experience, or she enjoys it. Not sure how to feel about a kid *enjoying* a fast food job, but whatever.

Anyway, my feelings about Jacky are strong enough to distract me away from finding Zandra Adams. Guess it means I'm grieving him already. Premature, but... hunch. People who intend to fight don't decline so fast. In the ICU room, he looked as brittle as someone who'd been battling cancer for months. Not even two hours earlier, healthy as a moose.

Wait...

Something supernatural is involved with Zandra's disappearance. Could they have gone after Jacky to distract me from tracking them down? Possible, but doubtful. Why would a powerful entity have an interest in a not-quite-famous screenwriter? I can't think of any reason she'd be significant enough to—oh, crap.

Could she be a creator?

Right as the thought hits me, my phone rings.

It's Kingsley returning my call.

"Hey," I say, trying hard not to sound like I'm teetering on the verge of crying.

"Sorry I didn't pick up before, was in the middle of a deposition. I'm *mostly* certain my client didn't do it."

I give a halfhearted chuckle. "Always a plus. So... umm..."

"Uh oh, sounds bad already."

"It is." I explain the situation with Jacky. "Would you be able to do whatever legal stuff is needed for me to manage Jacky's estate if his will doesn't specify some other executor? I found a lawyer's contact information in his address book. Guessing if he has a will, she'd know about it."

"Whoa. You think he's going to die?" asks Kingsley.

"Not necessarily from a supernatural sense. I teleported him to the hospital literally seconds into the heart attack, and he *still* ended up comatose in the ICU. If I hadn't been there with him at the time, he'd definitely have died on the floor in the gym before an ambulance got to him." Feeling guilty, I bite my lip. If not for me being there, maybe he wouldn't have had the attack at all. Pretty sure his shadow-boxing didn't help, even if I didn't swing back at all. Then again, if I hadn't shown up, he'd probably have continued trying to lift the heavy bag and triggered the attack, anyway.

"All right. I'll do some reading. Estate law isn't my niche, but I'll help as much as possible. You should probably call his lawyer. Looks better than you having another lawyer contact her."

"Yeah. Okay. Thanks. Will do."

We talk for a while about random stuff, mostly him trying to cheer me up.

"No idea why this is affecting me so much," I say. "Not like I spent lots of time with him or went to his house for holiday meals or anything."

"Well..." Kingsley sighs. "You don't exactly have a ton of mortal friends. Makes them precious."

"True. Okay, let me get back to work."

"Dinner later?"

I smile. "Okay. Your place or out?"

"Why don't we go somewhere so we can spend our time talking rather than cooking or cleaning up after ourselves?"

"But if we go out for food, I'll need to wear pants."

"Hmm. You make a compelling argument."

Kingsley chuckles. "Oh… anything for me to start with regarding Jacky?"

"Not really. I couldn't find any next of kin. No records anywhere in the gym. I found an address for his apartment, but haven't checked there yet. Remember the funeral for his wife last year? Only twenty something people showed up, all friends of hers or gym regulars. No relatives. Dug as deep as I could go and found nothing."

"Damn, that's rough. Are you okay?"

"Yeah, as okay as I can be. Getting the grief over with now so if it happens, I'll be able to keep my head on straight and deal with everything."

"He might pull through," says Kingsley.

He might… and I might pull Zandra Adams straight out of my butt. Okay, pessimism isn't like me. "I really could use some cheering up. Got a case kicking my ass, too."

"Do tell."

"Already told you about it. Remember me asking about the funny aura on the one guy?"

"Oh, that."

"Yeah." I sigh. "It's like the universe opened up and swallowed her. The black van drove off into another dimension."

He laughs. "Don't joke about it. Might be

exactly what happened."

I groan. "Okay. See you in a few hours."

After we end the call, I reluctantly get off the sofa. Houses don't take care of themselves. Might as well deal with laundry first. It's probably strange of me to not even consider hiring a maid service or something since I have the means to do so now. Nah, it's not strange. It's me. Maybe some people can grow up too poor to own shoes as a child and be comfortable being waited on later in life. Not me.

Especially considering all the crazy in my life, doing such normal things as laundry and cleaning the house is a much-needed dose of sanity. Fortunately, Anthony outgrew his phase as the Michelangelo of skid marks… or maybe I should say Jackson Pollack. Some of the disasters I found in the laundry bin made the idea of diving headfirst down the throat of a huge dragon seem like a reasonable alternative to touching them.

Predictably, Tammy's bedroom is in complete shambles. Her wardrobe is somewhere between light goth, grunge, and metalhead, nothing overly fancy or girly. I mean, she *has* a few dresses but they mostly stay in the closet for special occasions. Suppose I should probably get on her case like most parents would to clean up her room, but I don't. Mostly because it's pointless to start an argument over something so trivial. If I'm going to start a conversation with my daughter that's going to end with doors being slammed, it's going to be over something far more serious than a messy floor. Life threatening type stuff. The time we've got on any one iteration of reincarnation is brief. We could all die at any minute and I don't want my daughter's last words to me to be 'I hate you' because I pestered her about a pile of clothing on the floor.

As long as her mess doesn't spill out into the hallway, it's her mess to live in.

But, I do pick her clothes up for laundry. Since I can't tell what's clean and what isn't, it's all going in the wash. She has a hamper, which does contain *some* articles of clothing. Several pairs of her jeans and a few shirts smell like pot smoke. Hard to say if she smoked it or merely hung out with people smoking. As far as I'm concerned, it's less harmful than alcohol. She knows I worry about her overdoing either, but she also knows I'm not going to come down on her for anything short of being actively reckless in regard to her life or others. Like, if she gets drunk somewhere, I'll let it go as a learning experience. But if she tries to drive while drunk, yeah, I'm going to lose my shit and she knows it.

She doesn't have to hide stuff from me, so she has no reason to do stupid shit.

Like drinking and driving. Ugh. Can't think about it. I'll curl up in the fetal position for hours on end, and I've got a job to do.

I suspect she and Kai are about to take their relationship to the next level. As much as I hate to think about it, she *is* eighteen now. If she tells me about it, okay. If not, okay. I'm here for whatever she wants to confide in me. My mother wouldn't have batted an eyelash if I brought a boy home and did the deed right in my bedroom. Dad would've raised hell—if by some miracle he noticed or was even there and not on the road.

No, it never happened. First time for me was in college. I went through grade and most of high school being 'that weird, dirty poor kid' no one paid much attention to. Somewhere during my junior year, I was accused of being 'hot.' Not sure how I changed overnight, but whatever. Had a couple boyfriends back then, nothing serious enough for clothes to come off, though.

Anyway… I pick up Tammy's 'floor closet.' Even though she's eighteen, doing this lets me pretend a little bit like I'm taking care of my little girl. I won't get to do this for her much longer before she moves out... though, given the economy these days, she might decide to stay for a while. Rent is not cheap and Gen Z-ers without rich parents have about as much chance of affording a home as I do of reincarnating after death.

Okay, maybe not quite as bad, but still. I wouldn't fault her for wanting to save money by staying here and going to a college close enough to drive to. Dammit, there I go again, hoping she does what would make *me* happy. Not like it's a problem for me to visit her if she goes out of state. Hell, she could attend university in freakin' London and visiting her is a few seconds of teleportation away.

Okay, that thought actually calms me down.

My son's room is too neat for a soon-to-be sixteen-year-old boy—except for his computer desk. He doesn't do the clothes all over the place thing. Anthony's deal is bags of snack chips, soda cans, Hot Pocket wrappers, and all manner of paper plates piled high around his computer area. Danny used to be bad for leaving mostly finished sodas (or beer) cans here and there and forgetting them. I wonder if Anthony, desk notwithstanding, is naturally neat or if Danny being inside his head pesters him about cleaning up. Damn the boy can eat, but he's not even close to fat. Either he's got a ridiculous metabolism or, like me, our supernatural nature has frozen our body size. Maybe every excess calorie he consumes gets turned into eruptive gas rather than fat.

It would definitely explain so much.

Most people would probably tell me my kids are old enough to clean up their own messes, and I shouldn't be tidying their rooms for them. Sets a bad example or something. Gets them used to having someone there to do it for them. I dunno. Maybe I'm subconsciously trying to encourage them to stay longer. Honestly, it soothes me to take care of them. I'm their mom. It makes me happy to be there for them.

After gathering all the laundry from our three rooms, I lug it out to the damn garage—maybe I *will* spend some money to hire contractors. Tear this annoying thing down and rebuild an attached garage. While sorting clothes, my mind wanders around all the nothing I've been able to find on Zandra. She doesn't have any enemies. No one has made threats to her, to her daughter, Greta, or to any of the studios she's worked for. A group of religious people tried to get one of her earlier movies banned because it depicted priests and nuns as a secret order of monster hunters who all carried weapons under their vestments. Dunno what their problem was, really. The movie made them out to be total badasses.

But yeah, other than the one incident with the movie *Night Priest*—cheesy as hell title—Zandra Adams has gone through life relatively unscathed. Most people have more enemies than her by the time they're out of high school.

I did find some annoyed fan mail about the unmade sequel to *Vampire Fiona*. None of it rose to the level of threat, purely fans wanting more. A few did make unserious threats against studio executives, producers, and the Oscar judges... such as, wanting vampires to bite them.

No demands, though. And no contact to her daughter, Greta, with a ransom request.

Once I've got the first load of laundry in the washer, I head back into the house and start cleaning, not so much because it needs it, more to keep myself busy. If I sit still, worry about Jacky and the Zandra case is going to drive me nuts. Honestly, I should be doing something to find her. Okay, wait. Maybe there is something I can do. It's basic and probably pointless, but more likely to find her than washing my floor.

From my office, I start placing calls to various police departments, starting with Corona PD and expanding outward in a spiral. Each time, I identify myself, explain I'm attempting to locate a missing person, give them a summary of the details, and ask if they've seen her or maybe found an elder Jane Doe wandering about with no memory of who she is.

A long while of nothing later, I take a break to move wash to the dryer and start the next load, then check in on Anthony. He's still got the game on, but is only using it to chat with friends while doing homework.

"You okay?" I ask.

"I guess. You?"

"I guess."

We trade weak smiles.

"Kingsley invited me to dinner tonight. I can stay here if you'd rather."

"It's okay, Ma. I'm dealing." He leans back in his chair. "And Dad's been trying to cheer me up. He mentioned a ritual that might help, but doesn't think you'd approve."

"Probably not if it's the same type of thing responsible for his present state. Jacky's got no need to hide from the Devil. Honestly, your father didn't either. He hadn't gotten deep enough into it for the demons to notice him."

Anthony squirms. "I know. It's not why he did it."

"Let me guess: he didn't trust me enough to die. Wanted to stay around to keep an eye on you and Tammy."

My son's guilty expression gives him away. Yeah, Danny must have told him exactly that… hopefully along with an apology for thinking me a threat to them, but I'm not gonna hold my breath.

"He says you're more like an angel now. You don't look dead anymore."

"Gee, thanks. You say the sweetest things." I sigh out my nose. "I'm talking to him, not you."

Anthony gives me a thumbs-up.

I head back to my office intending to continue calling police stations. Honestly, it's futile. If a vampire or some other supernatural being took Zandra, the police aren't going to be of much help. They aren't equipped to handle us, nor do they have jurisdiction in higher dimensions.

My phone rings. Ooh, maybe one of the detectives got something. Or it's Sherbet.

Uh oh. The caller ID reads St. Jude Hospital.

I swallow, take a deep breath, and swipe to answer. They're calling to tell me he's awake, right?

"Hello?"

"Am I speaking to Samantha Moon?" asks an older-sounding woman.

"Yes."

"I'm Rita Larson from St. Jude Medical Center. We have you as the contact person for Mr. Jacky O'Brien?"

"Yes, that's right."

"Are you the daughter or granddaughter?"

"No. A family friend. Jacky doesn't have any relatives I'm able to find."

Rita pauses. "I see. I'm very sorry to be the bearer of bad news. Mr. O'Brien has passed away."

I bow my head. "Damn…"

Chapter Seven
Shouldn't It Be Raining

The kids and I sit on folding chairs, watching a Roman Catholic priest talk about death.

I'm sure the guy's given the same speech hundreds of times to thousands of people. At least he sounds as if he knew Jacky, adding some personal touches to an otherwise boilerplate eulogy. Tammy fidgets constantly. Not sure if it's wearing a dress or death, in general, putting her on edge.

Jacky's service is nice enough. Can't say I've spent much time on the inside of churches in my life. Admittedly, my brain wandered, again searching for an answer to why a soul would want to leave Heaven to reincarnate here again. Is there such a thing as too much of a good thing? So souls get... bored in heaven and want to hop down here for a little action? Then again, I was led to believe that living life here on this earth helps the Origin understand itself a little better. It's why we were created: to help the big guy in the sky understand who and what it is.

Other than me and the kids, the only other people here are Benny and Taz, the two guys who worked for him as trainers, and the priest. It's a fairly nice day for November, low sixties with a bit of a breeze.

"Feels like it ought to be raining," says Anthony in a quiet voice.

"Yeah." I peer up at the sky, clear and cloudless.

"Guess I watch too much TV. They always make it rain during funerals."

I put an arm around his shoulders. Anthony leans against me. He's at the edge of crying, but not quite past it. Tammy, of course, barely knew Jacky and kinda didn't want to be here. Despite her indifference/disinterest, she's red-eyed and dabbing tears from her face, due to her being affected by her brother's emotional state.

My daughter is somewhat interested in meeting my parents, but has little interest in seeing Danny's again. She's still resentful they helped him keep her and Anthony away from me when he tried cutting me out of their lives.

So, yeah. Tammy doesn't really have grandparents. She also doesn't seem to need or want them the same way Anthony did with Jacky. She's close to Mary Lou. Having a 'cool aunt' beats perpetually angry and judgmental (the Moons) or high and disinterested (my) grandparents.

The priest finishes his eulogy and commends Jacky's body to the earth. As the workers begin lowering the casket, the priest approaches us. I thank him for his kind words and time; we shake hands, and he heads off toward his car.

Watching the casket sink catches me off guard with the finality of it.

For a few minutes, I can't stop crying. My tears are, however, silent. Only Tammy notices. Anthony's and my emotions are making her cry, too, but she's giving me this 'what the heck are *you* upset for?' side eye stare. The answer is right there in my head for her to see: I have no idea. Kingsley could be right and losing one of my rare mortal friends hurts. Jacky had been an odd bit of normality in my life. He'd helped me deal with becoming a vampire without even realizing he did so. Maybe death as a concept makes me sad. Maybe I'm sad because it hurts to see Anthony sad.

Not only is Anthony heartbroken at losing his 'grandfather,' he's numb and a little scared after our meeting with Gloria Levine two days ago. Jacky *did* have a will. Turns out he left everything to Anthony. The gym, his belongings, and a modest savings account. He'd made the change after Mary died, as he had no other living relatives, not even third cousins.

Perhaps it's Jacky having been so alone that's getting me emotional because it makes me fear the same thing happening to me. The day will come when everyone I now know is dead—except maybe Anthony. He might be immortal, too. Not sure. Even Kingsley… werewolves live a damn long time, but they're not completely immortal. The relentless clock will eventually catch up to him, too. Assuming, of course, we stay together. No, we aren't having any problems, but most couples have to work hard to tolerate each other for sixty years, never mind multiple centuries.

Regardless of what the future holds for me, Anthony is now technically the owner of Jacky's Gym. It's in trust for him until he turns eighteen. I get to deal with the paperwork of running the place until he's of age. Anthony hasn't said much about it yet, but I suspect he's going to want to keep it open as a memorial to Jacky. I'd say having Danny in his head could help with the business aspect of it, but my ex-husband didn't exactly run his law practice—or that strip club—very well.

The three of us stand up once the workers have finished lowering Jacky into his final resting place beside Mary.

Tammy and I start walking toward the Momvan, but pause as we notice Anthony approaching the grave. The mom in me tenses when he steps right up to the edge, even though I know the fall couldn't hurt him.

Once again, my eyes well with tears as I watch my son say his last farewells to the man he'd come to love.

Chapter Eight
Communication Breakdown

For the most part, Anthony keeps it together.

Two days after the funeral, he's more or less back to his old self. Since he's still a kid in high school, I'm making arrangements with Gloria Levine to hire an interim manager to run the gym for now. No almost-sixteen-year-old can swing basically a full-time job as well as deal with high school and have any time left over for fun. And yes, he needs fun. I can't let him get wound too tight with work and school just yet. Having his own business is *way* more demanding on his time than flipping burgers or waiting tables.

So, we're looking to hand off the day-to-day

to someone else for the moment. Kingsley has a guy in mind: Emmett 'The Wall' Floyd. He's a former boxing champion who hasn't been doing much with himself lately. Won a couple of big matches in London... in 1956. So what if they happened to be illegal underground boxing events. Oh, he also looks like he's forty. Did I mention he's a werewolf?

According to Kingsley, despite the guy looking like a cross between a bald biker thug and a caveman, he's got a good heart. Tries to only eat people the world's better off without. Yeah, he's got an unfortunate taste for fresh meat, but enough control to settle for animals if no suitable prey is around. Goes without saying his dark master is not on Team Elizabeth.

Doesn't sound like a bad idea to have an experienced boxer running the place, and if Kingsley trusts him, we should be okay. Also helps he's a werewolf. All the associated 'weird stuff' that's bound to follow Anthony won't rattle 'The Wall.'

As far as my case finding Zandra Adams goes, I've taken to extreme measures. I even paid a visit to Dolores Brandt, a genuine psychic. Last time I saw her was soon after my change. She'd done a tarot reading for me years ago, and in hindsight, I think she might've predicted what happened with the Red Rider. Meaning, my change from blood-sucking vampire into whatever I am now. Of course, up until it happened, what she told me didn't make much sense.

Still, it made her seem credible in a way I can't say for most other psychics aside from Allison.

When I spoke with her a few days ago, Dolores said something confusing about my burden ending thousands of years before it started, an enigma from a place beyond imagination, and I'd need to confront myself to escape a prison of eternity. At least she implied I'm going to find Zandra, but didn't give me any clue as to where, when, or how. Since our meeting, I'd been kinda hung up on the whole 'eternity prison' thing, trying to figure out if it's a reference to my immortality or more literal.

Allison's been working with Millicent and whatever ghosts they can contact, asking them for help locating Zandra. They, too, haven't come up with much beyond a spirit claiming the 'ascendant ones' know about us. What is it about ghosts? Why don't they ever give straight answers? Maybe when spirit energy flows openly in the air rather than being constrained by the physical structures of a brain, it results in everyone sounding like fortune cookies.

Of all the ghosts I've met, only Millicent seems to have her crap together. Then again, she's more 'visiting spirit,' than ghost. Plus, she was and still kind of is a powerful witch. For all I know, she, too, figured out a way to defy death.

It's a little past noon and I'm not sure what to do next. The next logical step seems like it would be to make contact with any vampires in the area. Problem is, I haven't been part of 'the scene' and don't know many. Fang does, however. Maybe he can point me in the right direction, though talking to him will need to wait for sundown.

It's a little nerve wracking, to be honest. No idea how other vampires are going to react to me, especially since I *can* feed off them. Not that I plan to, but simply being able to is going to ruffle feathers. One common thread among vampires of a certain age is they adore being at the top of the food chain. Things might get interesting if they figure me out.

My phone rings. It's Detective Sherbet.

Oh, awesome. Finally.

I scoop the cell off the desk, swiping to answer as I raise it to my ear. "Detective! Just the man I've been hoping to hear from."

"Hey, Sam. Sorry to call you in the middle of the day. I need to talk to you about something important."

I blink. "Is it about the black van?"

"Can we meet somewhere? Rather not talk about this over the phone."

"Uhh, sure. Starbucks?"

"Yeah, that works. The one on Harbor? I'll head there now," says Sherbet.

"Okay. Same."

We hang up.

Damn, this doesn't sound like it has anything to do with a mysterious van.

The Starbucks in question is on the corner of Harbor and Chapman in downtown Fullerton. Fairly busy spot. However, there's a little red-brick passageway between the building it's in and the next one by this Ubatuba Acai place. People don't usually go back there, so it makes for a good teleport landing point.

Naturally, I make it to Starbucks before Sherbet. Might as well absorb some energy from people while here. It's a stupid thing to complain about all things considered, but this new psychic vampirism takes getting used to. As a bloodsucker, I only needed to feed a couple times a week. Now, it's more like four or five times a day depending on my stress level.

Used to be only taxing my supernatural abilities or being injured made me hungrier more often. Now, high levels of stress, anxiety, or focus do it, too. Makes sense, I suppose. Burning mental energy makes me hungry since mental energy is my food now.

Fortunately, I live in an area with loads of people.

Sherbet walks in a few minutes after I've taken a seat. Got myself a caramel macchiato and a grande black coffee for him. He doesn't do the fancy latte drinks, partly because he's trying to watch his weight and also because, as Denis Leary put it, he likes 'coffee-flavored coffee.' So, I have a plain black dark roast waiting for him.

Much to the objection of the buttons on his shirt, he sits. Seems his battle with donuts is ongoing, but he's at least not getting any bigger. He glances at the cup, nods at me, and proceeds to just stare into space.

Cops, even detectives, have a number of facial expressions in common wherein one does not need to have powers of mind reading to understand their thoughts. Common examples include: YGBSM face, also known as 'you gotta be shitting me.' The 'you're definitely getting a ticket' face. The 'you've really screwed up now' face, the 'why are we even here' face, and the one he's making now—the 'I really screwed up' face. Given what I know about him, it's improbable he's broken the law or committed a grievous error of the kind capable of sending a cop to prison or being fired for.

No, this one's likely personal—and there's only one topic I can think of with the power to render him unable to talk.

"Did something happen with Zayn?" I ask.

"Yeah. You can say that."

"I just did." I offer a reassuring smile. "How bad?"

Sherbet rakes a hand up through his hair. "I, uhh, walked in on Zayn and another boy."

I raise both eyebrows.

"They were only kissing," says Sherbet, unable to make eye contact. "I tried to be understanding and roll with it, but Zayn got upset and stormed out."

"Hmm. Why would he storm out if you were trying to play it cool?" I ask.

Sherbet fidgets at his coffee cup. "Note I said 'tried to be understanding.'"

"So, what happened?"

He sighs. "I might have stumbled over my words… stammered, generally made an ass of myself."

"So what happened?"

He sighs. "I dunno. I literally couldn't shut myself up. Everything that spilled out of my mouth made it worse. End result: he thinks I'm ashamed of him."

"Can I say something you're not going to like?"

"Might as well. Everyone else does."

"I think you *are* a little ashamed of him. Some part of you, the way you were brought up, looks at his being gay as a negative thing, an abnormal circumstance you wish didn't happen. Otherwise, you wouldn't get all quiet and awkward whenever it comes up."

He sucks in a breath to speak, but I hold up a hand to stall him.

"I'm not blaming you here. You're a product of your time and environment. I know you love your son. Believe me, I can see it in your head. Who are you trying to 'save face' for? Your parents? Other macho cops?"

"Yeah, I dunno." He pops the top off the coffee and takes a sip. "Been asking myself that same question the past two days. I haven't seen him since."

"He's been missing for two days?"

Sherbet nods. "Yeah. The guys are keeping an eye out, but he hasn't been to school either. I checked all his friends, anyone I even think knows him. None of them will talk to me. They all think I'm this gay-hating bigot who drove him out of the house."

"You're not." I grasp his hand. "You're a man who's trying to do the best he can for his son and struggling with how."

"I screwed up, Sam. If it will get him to answer his phone and talk to me again, I'd walk through the station in a pink speedo singing show tunes."

The absurdity gets a chuckle out of me. "Well, until you reestablish a relationship with him, he'd take it as you making fun of him."

"I know… just want him to come home. I'm worried about him." He looks at me with red eyes. "He needs to come home and be safe. None of his friends will tell me anything. The way he must talk to them about me, I'm sure they all think I'm happy he's gone. Please help, Sam."

"I'm on it. Got a list of his friends handy?"

"Yeah." He pulls a paper out of his shirt pocket and hands it over. "Thanks, Sammie. I can't even think straight right now."

I pat him on the shoulder. "I'll find him. Call you as soon as I have something."

Chapter Nine
Missing Persons

I walk Detective Sherbet out to his silver department sedan.

It's a lot nicer than the ones HUD issued me back in the day, but of course it's been over a decade. After he drives off, I stand on the sidewalk staring down the street. The Zandra case is bothering me in a way nothing else ever has. This is the first time in my career I've been at such a complete roadblock. There's usually at least one person with *some* information. Having vampire powers makes being a private investigator abnormally easy. It's basically cheating. That I'm *still* unable to get anywhere proves supernatural involvement.

Someone or something powerful has abducted Zandra Adams and covered their tracks well.

It's mildly reassuring to think about Dolores telling me I'll find her. Of course, she didn't specify the woman would be alive when I did. Alive was the implication, but it might also be my optimism coloring it.

Until Allison, Kingsley, or Fang run across a spirit or vampire with information, there's little I can think to do for Zandra at the moment. Zayn Sherbet is a more immediate, and hopefully much easier, problem.

I start off with the list Sherbet gave me of Zayn's friends from school.

The first friend on the list, Kristina Dwight, I find at her home two houses down from the corner of La Verne and Lemon Street. She's the same age as Zayn, seventeen, rail thin, and sporting long electric blue hair. Seems like a happy sort of person, at least until I mention the reason for asking to speak with her. Then she goes on the defensive.

This girl is highly protective of Zayn, treating him like a wounded little brother. It doesn't take me too long to convince her his dad is merely an idiot and didn't know how to talk to his son. An unintended benefit to being a vampire is getting to pretend to be younger than I am. Kids don't see me as forty-five (a.k.a. ancient and stupid) so Kristina doesn't filter out everything coming from my lips as nonsense.

Unfortunately, she doesn't know where he is other than 'safe.' Zayn's sent her a few texts but hasn't revealed his location to her out of worry his father would have cops give her a hard time. She, too, is worried about him missing school and doesn't think he should drop out because his father's an idiot. I do my best to reinforce the idea Detective Sherbet is really inept at emotional communication and absolutely does not hate his son.

I leave Kristina to the rest of her day, and her mom bewildered over why she let a complete stranger talk to her daughter for fifteen minutes.

Next up: Merritt Lindon. According to Sherbet's notes, Merritt is his son's best friend. They've known each other since grade school. I stop by his home address where his work-at-home dad tells me—after a little mental tweaking—he's at his job, which is apparently at a movie theater. Great. After lifting a mental image of what Merritt looks like from the father (spiky black hair with blond highlights, average build, lip ring), I head back to the Momvan and drive to the theater.

My frustrations with the Zandra case destroy any inhibitions regarding mental powers. I follow a breadcrumb trail of thoughts across the cinema complex to where fellow employees think Merritt is. As luck would have it, I find another of Zayn's friends, a purple-haired boy named Brandon Elder, working side-by-side with him cleaning a theater between screenings.

The pair look up at me as I walk in.

"Sorry, ma'am," says Brandon. "The theater's not ready yet."

"I'm not here to watch a movie. Are you Merritt and Brandon?"

The boys exchange a look, wondering if I'm a cop.

"Uhh, yeah," says Merritt. "Who are you?"

I insert feelings of trust into their minds. "I'm just a friend looking for Zayn. He's been missing for two days and his parents are worried about him."

Brandon scoffs. "His dad threw him out."

"No, he didn't." I sigh. "His father *is* a bit of an idiot in some regards, but he did not do that. He also doesn't hate Zayn. The man's simply got the emotional intelligence of a kumquat."

The boys chuckle, probably at the word more than the meaning.

"Heard different from Zay," says Merritt.

"Understandable. Both of them—father and son—can be stubborn. I've known his dad for years. So have you. I'm sure it hasn't escaped you Zayn is… flamboyant. His dad figured it out a long time ago." I look at Merritt. "You've seen the two of them together most of your life, right?"

He nods.

"Think about how his dad's behaved around you kids all these years. Have you ever seen him say or do anything hateful?"

"Nah. Just like… the dude is hella awkward. He'd get weird sometimes around us. Like you could see him wondering if me and Zayn were like in love or some shit."

"They're not," says Brandon. "Merritt's into girls… no idea why. They're so much work."

"He's right. We are usually a lot of work." I smile. "You guys have any idea where Zayn's hiding out? His dad's real worried about him and wants him to come home."

Merritt thinks about a youth shelter in downtown Fullerton, like four blocks away from the Starbucks where I met Sherbet. Okay. I'm a moron. Should have checked there first. I remember seeing something about there being a shelter in the area on the news a while back.

Apparently, some famous celebrity sponsors it. Can't remember who, though.

"Umm, not sure. Let me text him and ask if it's okay to tell you where he is."

"It's okay. You've done enough. Thank you."

Memories of me are erased from both boys. As they resume cleaning, I make my way out.

Chapter Ten
Safe Haven

The shelter is an unassuming building, technically on East Ash Ave rather than Harbor.

Looks like an ordinary—if large—home. The inconspicuousness is undoubtedly for the protection of the kids here, some of whom might be actively hiding from dangerous home situations.

I head up onto the porch and ring the bell. A thirtyish woman with a white brush cut answers a moment later. Her expression is pleasant but guarded. She thinks I'm either at the wrong house, a lawyer here to make trouble for someone, or a missionary of some kind.

"Yes?" asks the woman. "What can I do for

you?"

"Hi. I'm Samantha. I'm looking for a boy named Zayn Sherbet."

She folds her arms. "Doesn't sound familiar. Who are you with?"

"Officially, I'm a private investigator. Unofficially, a friend of the family. His father's asked me to help find him."

"Can't say there's anyone here by that name."

Grr. Okay, lady. Not in the mood for jumping through hoops. I hit her with a mental prod of trust. "Are you sure? His father's really worried about his son's welfare."

"Oh, um." She blinks, staring in confusion. "I, uh, suppose there's no harm in it. Yeah, he's staying here. Just arrived the other day. C'mon in. I'm Sharon." She leads me into what would've been a living room, only it's been converted into a small office. "Zayn's in room C."

"Thanks." I keep going into a hallway with three doors on each side and a bathroom at the end beside stairs leading up to a second floor.

Some of the doors are open, offering a view into rooms containing bunk beds. Room C's empty, though all of its eight bunk bed spaces appear lived in. I check room D, across the hall from it, in case someone there might have spoken to Zayn or seen him leave. The only present occupant is a girl in her teens with 'Marsha Brady' hair. She's pretty much the stereotypical 'California girl,' blonde, blue-eyes, pretty. My initial thought on seeing her is 'what's this kid doing in a shelter; she looks so normal.' Sigh. Not everyone has wild hair or clothes. An 'at risk' kid probably wouldn't come from an environment with loving parents. My best guess, she's no more than fourteen.

The kid's sitting on the lowest tier of a bunk bed, head down, absorbed in the contents of a beat-up computer tablet, most of her face hidden behind her hair.

"Hey," I say, trying to sound as casual and friendly as possible. "Have you seen Zayn recently?"

She looks up at me—and the breath catches in my throat. The whole left half of her face is covered in bruises and she's got a few stitches on her forehead.

Mom mode activated.

"Oh, sweetie… what happened?" I swoop in to sit on the empty bed opposite hers. It's all I can do not to squeeze her like an abandoned plush kitten.

Images of a screaming man appear in her

mind—her father's violent reaction to reading her personal journal. I'm expecting to see her run away in the memory flash, but the son of a bitch physically grabs her and throws her down the stairs, then picks her up off the landing and hurls her out the front door. She tumbles down the porch steps to the sidewalk and curls up there, in too much pain to move. The asshole bellows at her, screaming that she's not to come back, because he won't have 'one of those' under his roof. There's no mother in the memory, or any other voices shouting in the background.

Must control rage.

"Huh?" asks the girl. "Oh, my face.... you know, stuff happened."

"Who did that to you?"

"No one of any importance."

"You know, child abandonment is against the law. If your dad kicked you out of the house, he can get in serious trouble for it."

The girl gasps, staring at me, tears brimming at the corners of her eyes. "Who are you? How did you know that?"

"I'm good at reading people. And it really makes me angry when someone is mean to children."

"I'm not a little kid. I'm fourteen."

"Heh. You sound like my daughter at the

same age."

"Is she messed up, too?"

"You're not messed up, hon."

The girl looks at me again. "Are you my new therapist?"

"Not officially." I almost have to sit on my hands to stop myself from scooping her up and carrying her home. Just the way she's staring at me is tearing my heart out. I want to bring her home and adopt her. The only thing stopping me is worrying it's unfair to drag her into the weird supernatural world that comes along with knowing me. Still, this poor kid is going to gnaw at me for weeks. What's the point of having all this money if I can't take in an orphan or two? It does *not* help I'm staring down the barrels of empty nest syndrome. Two more years and I might have a house all to myself.

"Dunno why I'm even talking to you."

"It's good to talk sometimes. What's your name?"

"Paxton."

"That's a nice name."

She smiles and we talk for a bit about her situation. The police brought her here after the emergency room, so they're already aware of the home situation. She has no idea what, if anything, happened in regard to her father. It's probable he's been arrested already, or at least considered a danger to her if the police took her to this shelter. She's afraid of ending up in an abusive foster care situation and was planning not to come out to any foster parents.

Dammit. Hearing her anxiety over what horrible things foster parents might do to her is giving me anxiety. I *really* want to help this kid, even if it means fostering. But... I'd never forgive myself if something from my crazy, supernatural life ended up harming her.

"Here..." I hand her a business card. "Just between you and me, if you need help with anything, call me. Any time."

Paxton takes the card and looks it over. "A private investigator? But I don't need anyone investigated."

"I'm not offering you my services as a PI, thinking more along the lines of an angry mama bear." I look at the door, making an obvious show of not wanting to be eavesdropped on. "Sometimes, I work outside normal channels. Think of me as something of a guardian angel."

"I don't believe in that stuff. If I had a guardian angel, they'd have stopped my father from throwing me face first down the stairs."

Hearing those words gets me lunging across the space between beds and hugging her. It's tempting to go find this jackass and throw *him* down the stairs, but doing so would only turn me into the same kind of monster. I'm not, however, above compelling him to confess to the police.

Paxton sits there rigidly.

I'm about to let go since she doesn't seem to want to be hugged, when she clamps on and bursts into tears. Okay, this I *am* equipped for. I play mom for a little while until she calms down.

"So... if I end up in a bad place, you can get me out?"

"Yep."

"How? Are you a lawyer, too?"

"Nope. I was being slightly more than figurative when I said guardian angel. Can you keep a secret?"

She gives me the most hilarious 'bitch please' look I've ever seen. "Seriously? Dad had no idea about me until he read my journal. Heck, I'm not even sure about me. So what if I question things, was that such a big deal? My dad went nuts."

"Okay, so you can keep secrets. Think of any number."

Paxton narrows her eyes, clearly thinking.

"1,758," I say.

She blinks. "Whoa. How'd you do that?"

I smile, say nothing.

"Grr. Okay, then what color am I thinking about?"

"Lavender, but it's not your favorite color. You don't really even like it that much. You are the exact opposite of my daughter, Tammy. You adore pink."

Her jaw drops open. "Umm... what's the name of the kid who sits on my left in homeroom?"

"Was Terrell, but he transferred out. Now it's Chris. And he sounds like a self-absorbed jerk."

"Oh. My. Gawd," whisper-shouts Paxton. "That's amazing... and scary."

"Amazing and scary... I've been called worse." I wink.

She laughs. "Umm, so why are you looking for Zayn? Can't you just like 'find' him if you're psychic?"

"There's different kinds of psychic. I'm mostly the telepathic kind."

"Cool." She pulls her hair off her face. "He asked me to promise not to tell anyone. But I'm worried about him. He's even more freaked out about being homeless than I am, and he's older, too. I think he might wanna hurt himself."

"Do you know where he is now?"

"He said something about going to Hillcrest Park to think. Wanted to be alone, since there's a lot of people here."

Shoot. If Zayn truly believes his father hates him, no telling what he might do to himself. "Thank you for telling me. I need to find him before he does anything to harm himself."

She nods. "It's fine if you tell him I talked to you. I don't want him hurt."

"All right." I stand. "Remember, call me if you need anything, okay?"

"Okay. You're nice."

The words: 'If I had a mother, I'd want her to be like you' flit across her mind. Argh! If they ran youth shelters the same way they ran animal shelters, I'd carry this kid to the front desk right now and say 'I'll take her.' Calm down, Sam. This poor girl doesn't deserve to be thrown into a world of vampires, werewolves, demons, and who knows what else. Of course, she also didn't deserve to be literally thrown out of her house.

"I'd be proud to have a daughter like you."

"I didn't say anything."

I tap my head, and she reddens a little. "Oh, right."

"Don't lose that card." I point at her. "Any

time. For any reason."

"I understand. Thank you."

Summoning every scrap of willpower in me, I wave and leave the room. Anger knits the pieces of my cracking heart together. What kind of complete asshole throws his willowy fourteen-year-old daughter down the freakin' stairs? Making the mistake of looking at Paxton's memory of it, feeling her terror and heartbreak at being rejected has put me in a dangerous place mentally. Not gonna go looking for her father, but if I stumble across him, my soul might just get a bit of a dark stain on it.

Technically, I won't be murdering him. The ground will. It disturbs me somewhat to think how easily and subtly it's possible for me to kill now. Casually walk up to someone, touch them, teleport a thousand feet straight up...

And drop him.

Deep breaths.

Violent daydreams help deal with anger. Not going to act on it.

Instead, I need to find Zayn.

Chapter Eleven
This Place Again

In the interest of time, I teleport to Hillcrest Park.

It's beyond strange to be here. Used to jog around the park all the time. But now I mostly avoid it. Surprisingly, these surroundings don't trigger much of an emotional reaction. Seems I've dealt with my past enough not to feel much. Or years of keeping Elizabeth at bay has developed my ability to keep an iron lid on mental crap.

Not having much of an emotional reaction to the site of—basically—my murder bugs me more than being at the site where I died. Whatever. No time to dwell on any of my baggage now. I've got an eternity for navel gazing.

There are some moments in life where being an apex predator comes in handy. Like trying to find a person in the park. Fortunately, Hillcrest isn't exactly a dense, tangled mess of trees. I also know the area well. Vampire senses do speed up the process by helping me locate people rather than waste time canvassing every square inch.

I find Zayn west of the Hillcrest Rec Center, in a small patch of woods along Valley View Drive. He's sitting on the ground, back against a tree, unhurt, but visibly upset. The boy's slight of build, average height. He's got the same shade of dark brown hair as his father, but it's presently magenta in a weird style I'm too old to understand. Longish on one side, nearly shaved on the other.

Looks like he's been wearing the same outfit for a few days... probably stormed off right away without thinking, didn't pack. I dip into his mind. He's arguing with himself about going home, but doesn't want to stay. He's hoping to slip in, grab his stuff, and disappear without his father noticing him. Ugh. He really does think Sherbet hates him for being gay. He's trying not to hate himself, wondering if he really deserves his father's scorn for being a disappointment. Thoughts of running away scare him. He's feeling guilty about making his mother worry, but can't face his father again. Paxton's worries about him being suicidal thankfully appear to be a slight overreaction. He's just upset.

He spots me walking over and starts to get up. He's seen me a few times, knows who I am, and also figures his dad sent me.

"Hey, Zayn. Please don't make me run after you. Just here to talk."

"What are *you* doing here?" asks Zayn in a sassy sort of tone.

"Moonlighting as a therapist. Your father feels terrible."

Zayn relaxes, sits, and sighs. "Well, he should."

"Scale that back a notch, huh? You guys had a misunderstanding."

"Please…" Zayn rolls his eyes.

I sit on the ground beside him. "Your dad's an old-world cop. A man's man, as they used to say. Doesn't show his emotions much, and doesn't handle the awkward ones well at all."

"He sent you here to apologize because he can't?" Zayn tosses his head to throw his hair off his face. "Sounds like him."

"Your father asked me to find you because

he spent two days hunting for you, couldn't figure out where you went, and is completely messed up with worry." I look him in the eye. "You know how torn up he is? When he asked me to help find you before you got hurt, he actually cried. In public. At Starbucks."

"Yeah, right."

"Not big heaving sobs. One tear appeared but chickened out before falling." I smile, trying to cheer him up. "For him, that's pretty much like any other person breaking down."

"Why'd he say all that stupid stuff, then? I had to stand there in front of Seth while he cracked Richard Simmons jokes and made fun of us. I thought he at least liked me, but I guess he doesn't. Never told him I'm gay. Figured it was obvious enough, but I guess seeing proof was too much for him and he let me know exactly how he felt."

"No, Zayn." I rest a hand on his shoulder. "Your father loves you. Some people don't show their emotions much, and he's one of them. He still has emotions, though. The world he grew up in wasn't like things are now. People didn't talk about stuff like that."

"No excuse."

"No. Your father used to be afraid of how the guys at the station would react to learning he had a gay son. What he didn't realize is they all know already."

"Like, duh." He makes this fancy little hand motion. "Not like I hide it."

"Believe it or not, your dad once told me he'd break the jaw of anyone who gives you shit."

Zayn's mouth hangs open. "He did not."

"Yup. He's proud of you and right now, he's scared you're going to get hurt."

"You sure about that? Once, some jerks at school called me Rainbow Sherbet, and Dad heard them. We were going to a football game. Anyway, he looked ashamed of being seen with me."

"Hmm. Did he kinda angle his head down, and suck at his teeth, his right eye a little wider than the left? Like this?" I try to do my best Sherbet impression.

"Yeah, I suppose."

"Aha." I pat him on the shoulder. "Your dad wasn't ashamed. You witnessed him resisting the urge to go beat up a bunch of high school kids and risk getting kicked off the police force."

He scrunches his nose at me. "Really?"

"Yeah. I've worked with him often enough to know that look. Usually, he does it when a suspect he's interrogating isn't talking and he's forcing himself not to resort to a phone book."

"Huh?" Zayn tilts his head at me. "What the heck is a phone book?"

"Wow. You're making me feel old. Before the internet, they used to publish physical books listing phone numbers for everyone in a city. They tended to be fat... and heavy. It's an old cop cliché to beat suspects over the head with a phone book until they talk."

"Oh, ha. Pops would never do that. He's a good cop."

"He is. And when those idiots called you names, I'm betting he had to force himself not to at least get in their face and start yelling."

"Yelling at them would've made it worse, but I wanted him to."

"Got a feeling that if it happens again, he will," I say. "You running off really scared him."

"Then why did he make fun of me in front of Seth?"

"He didn't do it intentionally. Okay, you know how some kids at school are socially awkward and never seem to be able to say the right thing?"

"Yeah." Zayn wipes his eyes. He's been silently crying for the past few minutes.

"Your dad's basically that kid."

"But he's a cop. He's not afraid to say anything to anyone."

I playfully elbow him in the arm. "When dealing with suspects, sure. The man doesn't care what they think of him. He's afraid to say the wrong thing *to you*. He was raised to think a certain way, and he knows he's got some work ahead of him to set the old baggage aside. Your father loves you so much, he's terrified to say something stupid in front of you and do damage. And because he's so awkward, he says the stupid stuff anyway. Not gonna promise you he's done saying stupid crap, but please try to understand where it's coming from. He's basically a moose on rocket-powered roller skates, completely out of control."

Zayn laughs. "I can actually picture that."

"You know Paxton at the shelter?"

"Kinda. We like only just met. She ratted me out?"

"She thought you might hurt yourself. Not why I brought her up, though. Did she tell you how she wound up in the place?"

"Yeah."

"*That* is a father who hates his child for being different. Trust me, that son of a bitch hopes he never sees me."

Zayn gives me this impressed look. "You have always been kind of badass."

"Just kinda."

"So for real, my dad doesn't hate me?"

"For real." I glance off at the sky, pretending to be in deep thought. "Or is it 'for realz' with a z on the end?"

He laughs.

I stand. "C'mon. Time to go home."

"You're absolutely sure he doesn't hate me?"

"Positive." I hold out a hand.

Zayn stares at me for a few seconds before grasping my hand.

I pull him upright and teleport in one smooth move.

Chapter Twelve
A Few Issues

Zayn goes bug-eyed at the rapid change of scenery from Hillcrest Park to his front yard.

Before he can scream, I dive into his head and replace the memory of teleporting with an ordinary ride in the Momvan. Typical for a victim of vampiric mental surgery, he stares into space for a moment, then shakes it off and heads toward the house.

He pulls out his keys, unlocks the door, and goes in. "Mom? Dad?"

Something heavy hits the floor deeper in the house straight ahead roughly the same time Mrs. Sherbet yells "Zayn!" from an archway to the dining room on the left.

She arrives first, running over to hug him. Detective Sherbet races down the hall from the back of the house, also grabbing his son in a hug. This shocks Zayn. Sherbet senior isn't a big hug type person. One of those things 'men don't do' according to him.

"I said really stupid crap." Detective Sherbet pats Zayn on the back. "Can you forgive me?"

"Yeah, Dad."

"Oh, honey, you scared me to death." Mrs. Sherbet squeezes him, then leans back to look him over. "Are you okay? Have you been eating? Are you hungry?"

"I'm okay. Yeah, a bit hungry." He wipes tears. "I'm sorry, too. Said a bunch of nasty stuff about you to my friends. Gotta fix that."

Sherbet smiles. Yeah, his eyes are red. "Don't care what your friends think, or anyone. As long as you're safe."

"I left some stuff at the place, and really should tell Sharon I'm going home."

"The place?" asks Detective Sherbet. "Where were you?"

"Uhh, figured you'd check my friends' houses, so I spent the night in Hillcrest. Ran into this dude who told me about a shelter, went there to check it out and they let me stay."

"Shelter?" Detective Sherbet looks quizzically at me.

"There's a place for at-risk youth over on Ash," I say.

"Dammit. I should've thought to check there." He starts for the door. "C'mon. I'll drive you."

"Seriously? You'd want to be seen there?" Zayn raises both eyebrows.

He nods. "Yeah. I'm done giving a crap what everyone who isn't in this room right now thinks. Can't promise I ain't gonna say some dumb stuff in the future, but you are my son and nothing in this world means more to me than you."

Zayn breaks down again.

I can almost hear the rusty robot gears creaking as Detective Sherbet hugs him again. Yeah, it's going to take him a bit to get used to open displays of affection, but I think he's gonna manage. A moment later, when they've both collected themselves, they start for the door.

"Wait!" shouts Mrs. Sherbet. "Not before you eat. Why don't you go change out of those dirty clothes, have a nice shower, and we'll do an early dinner. Then you can go get your stuff?"

"Okay." Zayn makes a 'thanks, see ya

around' face at me before heading down the hall.

Detective Sherbet walks up to me, head down. "Thank you, Sam."

"Happy to help. Oh, did you have any luck with the partial plate on that black van?"

He tilts his head. "Black van?"

"Yeah, uhh, couple days ago I asked you for help identifying a black van involved in a possible abduction?"

"Hmm." Detective Sherbet stares at me with a complete look of bafflement. "Oh. Right. Sorry, it's been crazy. It slipped my mind to check on it. Dammit. I'll do it first thing tomorrow."

Strange. It's not like him to forget something. I peek into his head. Not out of suspicion he's lying, but worry someone messed with his head. He genuinely forgot about me asking, and feels horrible over it. Also, he can't figure out how he forgot.

This strikes me as some sort of suggestion, perhaps a subtle one.

"No problem. You had a lot going on with your boy. He needs you more than I do. Tomorrow's fine. Let me get out of here so you guys can have some family time."

Mrs. Sherbet thanks me profusely on my

way out the door.

Great. Now I'm not going to sleep. Whoever abducted Zandra somehow knows I'm involved and somehow knows I asked Sherbet for help. That is, if he's been told to purposefully forget my request. Maybe not. Maybe the detective is just getting old.

Then again, I suppose it could be worse. They could have straight up killed him. Ugh. As happy as I am to bring Zayn home in one piece, I'm too worried about my current case—not to mention whatever Elizabeth is up to these days—to really enjoy feeling happy for the Sherbets.

After all, the abduction case is just getting way too weird. I mean, why the hell is Zandra Adams so important? And why is she worth this level of concealment?

I didn't know, but I'm going to find out.

Chapter Thirteen
The Massacre at Victoria Drive

It's a little after ten on a Friday night.

I've melted into a Samantha-shaped puddle on my sofa, watching Judge Judy via streaming while overindulging on orange sherbet. Hey, I had the word on the brain, okay? Triggered a craving. Anthony's in his room playing his game. Tammy's out. She went to work after school and hasn't been home yet. She texted me at 7:04 p.m. to say she's leaving work and going to Veronica's place. Hasn't said anything since.

At 11:18 p.m., I send Tammy a 'where are you?' text.

At 11:36 p.m., I send another one, adding

'please answer.'

It's not like her to ignore my texts. Worried, I try a voice call. It rings for thirty seconds before hitting voicemail. After a second attempt to call her ends in voicemail, I try mentally shouting for her. I'm unable to project telepathic voices over long distances like she can. My power only works with direct line-of-sight. For her to hear me 'yelling,' she'd have to be listening to me at the time.

Anthony exits his room and crosses the hall to the bathroom, pausing to say, "Incoming! You might need a gas mask, Ma."

Lovely.

I send Tammy another text, asking her to let me know she's okay.

A noise rumbles out of the hallway that gives me a mental image of C'thulu beatboxing. Anthony laughs. I sincerely hope the day comes when a thunderous release of gas no longer amuses him to the point he needs to text his friends about how loud it was.

Whatever kind of immortal he's turned into, he still needs ordinary food—though not all of it agrees with him. My son adores broccoli, but not for the health benefits. He loves it for the volume of its aftereffects.

Again, I really hope he outgrows this.

I call Veronica's mother.

The phone rings for a long time before a sleepy woman asks, "Hello? Who is this? Do you have any idea what time it is?"

"12:09 a.m.," I reply. "It's Samantha Moon, Tammy's mother. She's not answering her phone or texts. Is your daughter home?"

"Uhh... hold on. I was in bed."

I listen as patiently as possible to the rustling of her getting up and staggering down the hallway, yawning. Anthony goes back to his room. I brace for stench; mercifully, the tainted air doesn't leave the bathroom.

"Ronnie's not in her room. She said something about going to a party tonight. Might be sleeping over at Paige's."

"Thank you. Sorry for waking you up."

She sucks in a sharp breath. "It's okay. Do you think something's wrong?"

"Tammy doesn't usually ignore texts or calls from me. Her phone's not dead since it's ringing. Maybe she lost the phone somewhere or she's asleep early."

"Oh, could be. Should I worry?"

I fidget. "Not yet... let me try Paige's house first."

"Okay."

A call to Paige's mother goes unanswered.

The second time I call, straight to voicemail. Okay, her parents are not happy about being disturbed after midnight. Guess they're not awake enough to recognize my name on the ID.

Dammit.

I stare at Judge Judy's paused face for a few minutes, trying to think of my next step. Her imaginary voice in my mind says 'don't just sit there, do something.' Teleportation isn't going to work here since I haven't been to either one of her friends' houses. Also don't know which one she might be at. *If* they're even still at any of them. 'Party' could mean they've gone to some other kid's place, not one of her friends.

Blargle...

I gasp. "Tammy?"

My daughter's voice manifests in the back of my mind again... except she's not really speaking, more like babbling.

"I can hear you. Are you in trouble?"

Mmmoooomm... oh, gawd.

"What happened?"

We beered too much drank. Tired and the floor is soft. Some driving nobody.

Oh... whew. My kid's blind drunk. Not kidnapped by supernatural forces.

Not blind. I can see. Want home. Can't sleep.

Weird. Drunk usually knocked me right out.

Nnn. Can't sleep... here. Don't trust boys.

I stand. "Where are you?"

House.

"Whose house?"

Run's house.

"What?"

She starts mentally singing *Whose house? Run's house* over and over between laughing.

"Tam... where is the party?"

Uhh. Gotta look at my phone. Can't do it when we're talking.

"You're not talking to me with your phone."

Oh. Yeah. You're right. Gimme a minute.

I run down the hall to Anthony's room. He's on the computer. "Ant."

He pulls his headphones off one ear. "Yeah?"

"I need to run out and pick Tammy up. Keep an eye on the house, okay?"

"No problem."

Mom.

I hurry down the hall and out the door to the Momvan. "What's the address?"

Yeah. Wanna go home. Umm. It's on my phone.

"You have your phone out?"

I do. It's glowing. She giggles in my head.

How'd they make these so small? It's like a whole computer in here and it's so small.

"C'mon, Tam Tam. You're at a party and you don't want to sleep there because you don't trust the boys. Where are you?"

Oh, umm... She rattles off an address on Victoria Drive.

"On my way."

***

I pull up to a fairly ordinary house, except for there being a half-dozen high school kids unconscious on the lawn.

"What the hell?"

How the heck have the cops not shown up yet? I park, hop out, and run over, checking the kids—all boys—over for signs of serious problems. None of them look to be in serious trouble, only sleeping.

The front door isn't fully closed due to a girl's arm being in the way. She's probably a senior, looks cheerleader-y. I pull her inside. Don't want anyone slamming the door on her arm and breaking it.

I find an absolute massacre in the living room. You know those movies they made in the Eighties where some kid's parents go away and a bunch of the friends show up for a party that trashes the place? Yeah. Someone is going to be grounded until they're done with college. There have to be sixty or more teenagers laying around like a Civil War reenactor group at the end of a battle. Some are draped over the sofa, some sprawled on the floor. One boy's hanging off the upstairs balcony, bent over the railing. His puke's splattered on four or five kids unconscious on the floor beneath him.

"What the actual fuck is going on here?"

Plan time. Step one: check for emergencies. Step two: load my kid in the Momvan. Step three: call this in to the police. Suspicious white dust on the coffee table freaks me the hell out. Looks an awful lot like someone had coke, and I don't mean soda. Maybe they simply cut E pills in half, or maybe it's coffee creamer, but dammit. It looks bad.

Mom? Kitchen.

I step carefully around bodies in the hallway. Everyone appears to be alive at least, even though it looks like an entire high school's worth of zombies got massacred in here. Tammy is curled up in a ball under the kitchen table. Two girls I don't recognize are *on* the table, unconscious. Red solo cups are everywhere. The back door is open. More kids are hanging out around a keg in the backyard, maybe seven or eight football players, none of whom have passed out yet.

They don't appear to notice me.

"Mom," whispers Tammy. "Can you give my friends a ride, too? You said I could always call. Didn't wanna let Veronica drive."

I grasp Tammy's ankle and drag her out from under the table, displacing beer cans and two other kids.

"Whoa," whispers Tammy. "The room is moving."

"Hey, kiddo." I pull her up to sit, looking her over. She's quite drunk but stopped before reaching the point it knocked her into a metaphorical coma.

"Mom." She smiles dizzily. "Please find my friends before you call the cops on us."

"Okay."

I place her seated in a chair and hurry around the kitchen, checking kids over for alcohol poisoning or obvious drug-related issues. Fortunately, none of them are in a state bad enough to worry me into immediately calling 911.

One by one, I locate Tammy's friends and carry them out to the Momvan.

Dana's on the kitchen floor. Ankita's hiding

in the closet. The poor girl's only 'two-beer-tipsy' but had a social anxiety attack and hid. When she sees me open the closet door, she grabs on and shakes like I'm saving her from a coal mine collapse after six days trapped underground. She gets a 'calm down' mental poke. Renee's sacked out in the master bedroom next to a boy who I vaguely recall dating her. No idea what if anything they did, don't wanna know. I find Paige hanging out the window of an upstairs bedroom, apparently belonging to a teenage boy. A long swath of vomit paints the siding below her. Ari's in the bathtub with two other girls, all fully dressed and sitting there having a delirious conversation. They seem more high than drunk, though it could be her personality. I peek into her head and don't see her using any drugs, just beer and wine coolers. Hmm. Ariana's the bubbly friend who laughs at everything. It seems alcohol makes her into a space cadet. I carry her out to the Momvan and give her a mental prod to sit still—unless she has to throw up.

I find Veronica on the floor in the living room. I find her shirt hanging off the ceiling fan. Easy enough to retrieve and put back on her. She's Gumby-level unconscious. Okay, when I told Tammy she could call me anytime, anywhere in a situation like this and I'd pretend nothing happened, I never expected to find her in freakin' Jonestown.

What is wrong with kids these days? Wow.

I carry Tammy out to the van, set her in the passenger seat, and buckle her in.

For the finale, I go inside the house one last time and call 911 from the phone there, leaving it off the hook. Some of those kids have obviously overdone it and probably need medical attention. That done, I drive Tammy and her friends back to our house. They can sleep it off here where I know someone—me—will keep an eye on them. Staying up all night only means I'll need to drain more energy tomorrow.

The ride home is relatively quiet. Tammy's awake but not talking. Ari randomly giggles to herself, but also doesn't say anything. The other girls are all sleeping. After parking in my driveway, I help Tammy out of the van. She's too inebriated to walk on her own.

"Sorry," she whispers.

"We live, we learn. Next party you go to, I hope you'll be a bit less aggressive."

"Yeah. I had too much." She wobbles, grabbing me for support on the way to the door. "I didn't let Veronica drive. She wanted to go home like at eleven, but she couldn't even walk.

She almost did anyway, but I refused to get in the car, so she stayed. Sorry. I screwed up."

"It's okay. I'd rather have you drunk and call me at whatever late hour than end up dead on the road."

Tammy tries to hug me, misses, and goes spilling over. I catch her before she face-plants. She turns toward me, going for the hug again. Seconds before contact, her mouth opens, releasing a spew of puke.

My vampire agility kicks in. Like something out of *The Matrix*, I duck, twisting out from under the spray of horribleness, and pop back up behind her, holding her so she doesn't fall into her own mess.

"Oops," says Tammy after coughing. "Didn't mean to... Mom?"

"Right here."

"How'd you get behind me so fast?"

"Duh. Mother's reflexes."

She laughs.

"C'mon, kiddo. It's past your bedtime."

Tammy pretends to cry like a four-year-old. "But I wanna go to bed."

"Yes... yes, you do."

Anthony appears in the door. "Whoa. She's obliterated."

"Ant? Help me out here? Her friends are in

the van."

"Sure, Ma."

Between the two of us, we get Tammy and her friends inside.

It's gonna be a long night.

Chapter Fourteen
Sebastian

I didn't stay up *all* night, only most of it.

By around five in the morning, it seemed Tammy and her friends had gotten through the worst of it and none of them had a medical emergency. We'd arranged them on the living room floor with blankets, pillows, and comforters somewhat like the sleepovers she had a few times in her tweens. I set out a couple pitchers of water and a bottle of headache pills on the coffee table before letting myself fall asleep on the couch beside a row of smartphones.

Ari woke me a little after nine. She bounced awake and other than a mad sprint for the bathroom to let the beer out, didn't behave as though anything unusual happened last night. The old saying opposites attract doesn't always apply to romance. Tammy's an odd combination of overly mature, quiet, grim, and even morbid on occasion. Ari is basically the avatar of happiness. She somewhat reminds me of a less hyperactive Mindy Hogan, the one-time zombie.

Unaware I'm awake, Ari returns from the bathroom, helps herself to a glass of water, then looks around. "Whoa. Someone changed the house."

The look of complete bewilderment is too much for me, and I crack up.

She jumps, hand over her heart, staring at me. A few seconds later she blurts, "Oh, you scared me, Ms. Moon."

"Sorry." I sit up. "How do you feel?"

"Fine, why?"

"Because you guys got wrecked last night."

She waves dismissively. "I only had like three beers."

The phones start going off, so I play receptionist, talking to parents and letting them know their daughters spent the night here. Ankita's parents want her to go home as soon as she wakes up. I tell Paige's mother her daughter probably had a 'never again touching beer' type night. Of all Tammy's friends, she looked the most inebriated. Takes talent to be the girl who pukes out the second story window.

Tammy doesn't stir until a little after ten. She pushes herself up, peels the stuck pillow off her face, and gives me this look part way between embarrassed and grateful. As promised, I don't intend to give her grief for drinking at a party, even though I'd prefer she didn't. Mostly, I think about being proud of her for refusing to get in the car with Veronica and making such a scene her friend decided not to drive.

She slinks off to the bathroom.

By noon, everyone's awake and picking at a plate of toast I set out for them. My living room smells like beer burp, toast, butter, and jam. Paige and Renee still seem a little tipsy. I make sure they drink enough water. Tammy sits next to me, still more embarrassed than anything. She hasn't said or telepathically sent anything to me, but I suspect she regrets losing control and drinking too much. Drinking until passing out seems to be a rite of passage for most people. Hopefully, she doesn't make a habit of it. Though I can't see Anthony doing it. Danny had the occasional drink or two, but as far as I can remember, never became drunk during the time I knew him.

Eventually, the girls are well enough to go outside.

Once again, I play chauffeur, driving them home. Veronica's parents can deal with helping her get her car back from the party site. I don't mention anything about the police likely showing up there, but I'm sure Tammy knows. She would also understand I did it out of concern for the kids' health, not to get anyone in trouble. Someone is almost certainly going to get in trouble, but it's an unavoidable necessity.

When I get back home, Tammy's in her bed and the hallway smells like a recent shower. Anthony's already cleaned up the living room, putting all the blankets, comforters, and pillows away. Wow, this kid. He left me a note saying he went to Topher's to hang out. Pretty sure Tammy's going to be recovering all day.

Okay, crisis managed.

I pull out my phone to call Sherbet, intending to follow up on the black van... but notice a reminder on the screen that reads: Sebastian 1:30. Under normal circumstances, I'd be late as it's presently 1:22 p.m. No mortal can get from Fullerton to Laurel Canyon in eight minutes without a supersonic aircraft.

Given the Zandra case hanging over me, I

really ought to cancel with Sebastian today, but it's not like I have any leads to follow up on yet. Sitting at home being frustrated totally won't help. I change into a T-shirt and loose military-style pants, then teleport to the bathroom at Starbucks. It's a nice hidden landing spot, but does occasionally offer awkward moments, like now.

Appearing out of nowhere in front of a woman sitting on the toilet is something of a shock for her. I zap her in the brain before she can scream, making her forget seeing me. While she stares into space amid a mental fog, I let myself out of the room. Getting so little sleep has made me hungry. All the customers waiting in line start yawning together. I exclude the baristas since the job is mentally draining enough without a psychic vampire making it worse on them.

After buying a mocha latte—pretty sure coffee doesn't actually help me wake up, but there *is* a noticeable placebo effect—I duck into the back hallway by the bathrooms and teleport to Sebastian's place.

It's not quite an estate per se, though it's a large house on a good amount of property. He likes having a bit of privacy. So, why am I here? Well, it *is* work-related in a way. Months ago when we went on our grand European vacation, Fate decided not to let me get off easy. Something bizarre happened everywhere we went, like I'm some kind of supernatural calamity magnet.

Hey, yanno… 'supernatural calamity magnet' would kinda work as a rock band name.

Anyway, when we visited Denmark, my daughter fixated on this statuette of Freya—yes, the goddess—which turned out to be some kind of conduit for the goddess to communicate with mortals. To make a short story shorter, Freya chose Tammy to be her temporary avatar on Earth and cleanse a defiled old temple. We got into a fight with magically preserved Viking warriors who raised the concept of 'stubborn' to an art form. Not even the Devil Killer put them down permanently. Came as a shock to me, but Allison figured out why. See, the sword Azrael gave me can kill anything *alive*. Even the Devil. Angels aren't given to being terribly poetic, so when they made a sword to kill the devil, they named it the most logical thing to them.

Anyway, those Nordic zombies were neither true zombies nor alive. Allison thinks they worked more like golems. Some kind of magical curse animating desiccated flesh, somehow infused with the skills of ancient swordsmen.

Not true souls. 'Killing' them required destroying the curse, not destroying a life, ghost, or soul.

I'd used the Devil Killer relatively often up to that point, but there's a big difference between attacking an unarmed or unskilled person—or demon—with a sword and going up against what had likely been some of the best fighters of their day. This is a guess on my part as to how those particular men ended up being chosen to 'guard' the temple site.

Point being, they kinda handed me my ass. I spent the whole time on the defensive. If I hadn't possessed vampiric strength and speed, they would've killed me in less than twenty seconds. If not for Freya temporarily empowering my daughter, we'd probably *still* be in that room. Watching my then-seventeen-year-old daughter whip a Viking blade around like something straight out of a *Lord of the Rings* movie further made me feel like a cavewoman clubbing at bad guys.

So... figure if I'm going to pretend to be a demon-slaying angel, I might as well learn how to use a sword properly. California has a surprising number of 'professional' sword-fighters. However, they all presented the same basic problems: they are mortal and they mostly work with film crews or stunt performers. Meaning, they teach how to make a swordfight *look* good, not so much actual technique. Their being mortals is an issue because I'd constantly be resisting the urge to take advantage of superhuman speed, and probably wouldn't learn much anyway.

Fang helped me out by putting me in touch with this man, Sebastian Bulle.

He took this name a century or two ago, though I haven't a clue what name he lived under as a mortal. Yes, he's a vampire. No, he's not on Team Elizabeth. Good thing, that. He's pretty old. See, Sebastian was around when people still fought wars with swords. He'd been a commoner when alive, which put him right on the front lines of a handful of feudal battles in the 1600s. Nothing historically significant though, mostly spats between landowners in France.

For the past few months, he's been gracious enough to work with me on sword fighting techniques. Considering he's 400 years old as a vampire, I'd expected him to be much faster than me. He is, but not to the degree I anticipated. Generally, vampires become more powerful the longer they exist. My mere fourteen years as an immortal should have made our sparring match feel like I'm the normal human trying to fight my vampire self.

Not sure if psychic vampires—or whatever exactly I've become—break the power curve, or if Sebastian is going easy, weaker than average, or elders don't increase in power as fast as my assumptions dictate. He enjoys being an enigma and hasn't answered my questions about it.

Regardless of the why of it, he's still faster and stronger than me and it makes our sessions meaningful. After years of having a big advantage over humans I've been forced to fight, I kinda hate feeling like the slow, weak student struggling to keep up. However, it's also necessary. The easy path doesn't teach much.

Sebastian's assistant—they both dislike the term butler even though it's basically what the man does—James meets me at the door and escorts me down to the basement studio, which looks like a cross between a prestigious fencing school's gym and a medieval warfare scholar's museum. The vast room is lined with hundreds of different swords, armor suits on stands, and even a few authentic tapestries that once hung in legit castles.

"Good afternoon, Sam," says Sebastian, in perfect English, no accent. He's standing in the middle of the sparring area, hand on a thin practice longsword, point in the mat beside his shoe.

The man appears to be in his late thirties, despite having prematurely grey hair he wears long in a ponytail. He's a weird mixture of fierce and effeminate. I can't look at him without imagining him dressed in some old-timey costume with frilled cuffs and collar. As typical for vampires, he's got the pallid greyish complexion of a recently deceased corpse, and stark gold-colored eyes.

Despite his frightening look, he's surprisingly amicable. His raison d'être, as he puts it, is to enjoy existing and to exist for as long as possible. He adores anything he considers fun or whimsical, and—lucky for me—sword fighting is something he considers an entertaining pastime. Even his dark master, Akhenaten, has a fondness for good times. Yeah, his DM is kinda old, as in the man died around 200 BCE or something.

"Hi, Sebastian. Sorry I cut it so close today. Had kid issues."

"Oh, do tell?" He smiles, gesturing with his free left hand at the rack of practice swords.

They're essentially real swords, except for not being very sharp. Considering the speed and strength involved with a pair of vampires sparring, the lack of a razor edge isn't going to stop injury if I make a mistake... but we both heal pretty fast.

I explain the Tammy getting drunk situation while we get into a light exchange of strikes and parries. He catches me 'chopping' a couple times and *tsks*. It's a natural result of me picking up a sword without prior training. A person's first instinct is to basically hack with the sword at the bad guy. These longswords are primarily intended for thrusting, not overhead chops, though they're passable at slicing attacks. Weeks ago, he'd explained all about the evolution of the longer, thinner blades as a reaction to the development of chain mail armor. Precise thrusts had a much greater chance of breaking through the linked mail than slashes.

The Devil Killer is a medium-sized blade, somewhat shorter and wider than a traditional longsword, but it's also not as big as a 'classic' broadsword. Sebastian has been training me in a mixture of longsword and broadsword styles, but still makes faces at me when I thrust the broadsword or hack the longsword.

Once I'm finished explaining what happened with Tammy, our session escalates into superhuman territory. The dark wood-paneled room and all its hanging swords becomes a background blur as we go after each other at ever-increasing speed. Any human in the room would see only a blur along with a continuous banging of steel on steel like an ingot stuck in a fan.

Sebastian consistently stays a little ahead of me, but I do land a hit roughly once for every three times he 'kills' me. Each time he taps me with a strike that would've been fatal to a mortal in a real fight, we pause the sparring to go over what I did wrong and how I should've reacted.

The pace is pretty punishing. No mortal could go at this intensity for four minutes let alone two hours, but despite its lethal necessity, I find it fun as well as relaxing in a 'blowing off stress' way. After only basically five months, it already feels like a re-match with those Nordic zombies wouldn't be so one-sided. I still couldn't kill them permanently, but I wouldn't spend the entire time retreating from one guy.

When our session ends, we move from the studio to the adjacent room. He's decorated it in the style of a medieval castle's dining hall—albeit much smaller. Giant, rectangular table, big chairs with red velvet cushions, more tapestries, and so on. Being in here could easily convince someone they fell through a hole in time.

He hands me a glass of wine—since I don't

do the blood thing anymore—then fixes a goblet of blood for himself before joining me at the table. I've already told him about the Red Rider and my 'change.' Had to get it out of the way soon after we met when I first passed on his offer of blood. We spend a few minutes talking about highlights from the past few hours of sparring.

"You are learning quite well, Samantha." He smiles. "It is so nice to have someone who appreciates the old ways. Vampires today have become too enamored with technology. Firearms are so graceless."

"Thanks. I'm starting not to feel like I have to think about every move."

He nods. "Yes. One must react by what they call muscle memory and instinct. If you are thinking about how to defend or attack, you'll be too slow. Keeping up practice is the only way to stay sharp."

"As long as you're willing to have me over, I'm happy to be here. This is surprisingly fun."

He twirls his hand while bowing. "There is no other point to existence but to enjoy the ride."

I'd comment about not everyone seems to understand this philosophy—and some people are downright miserable—but he knows. The mortal life he once led in 1600s France makes even homelessness in modern America seem like paradise.

"Mind if I ask you something unrelated?"

He holds his goblet out to me. "By all means. Conversation is another of my many pleasures."

"I've been trying to find a woman who was abducted under strange circumstances, and I'm coming up completely empty handed. It's incredibly frustrating." I explain the Zandra situation. "No one seems to know what the thin shimmering aura is. It's not like an 'aura' in the traditional sense, more like the way the sun forms a shimmer around the moon during an eclipse. Almost like a ghost was standing superimposed over him. Do either of you have any thoughts on what the aura might mean?"

I find myself talking to both Sebastian and his dark master, who, I know, is listening in on this conversation. It's apparent because the swordsman's eyes occasionally flash fire... a true indication of a lurking master. I still haven't quite figured out if Akhenaten forcibly took Sebastian over or if they have a rapport. Considering their cordiality, I suspect they're content with their arrangement.

Sebastian swirls a tiny bit of blood around

his glass, staring into it as the joviality melts out of his face. After a moment, he speaks in a voice more than an octave deeper, thick with an Egyptian accent. "It reminds me of our apparitional selves in the Void. There, we took on our human visages, tattered, devoid of color, and shrouded in restless spiritual energy. It is possible you saw a dark master briefly possessing a human without binding to them. Though I have not witnessed this in person, I understand the theory of it. Up until the Void ruptured, such a thing was not possible. A dark master would need to be out and about in this realm in order to do so. Previously, our only path to freedom occurred via traditional possession."

"So, now that the dark masters have spilled out of the Void and can roam the mortal world like ghosts, they can possess people whenever they want?" I ask.

"In theory," says Akhenaten. "It would be far from ideal. Such a possession would impart only a fraction of their power. They would not be significantly stronger, faster, or tougher than an ordinary human. Other than serving as spies or for reasons of subterfuge, there is little point to it."

"This guy mind-controlled Zandra, though. Whatever he is, he still has some powers."

"It is telling that the 'seeing machine' revealed him. This means he is clearly not an ordinary vampire."

He's talking about the security camera. I shift my jaw side to side, thinking. He's right. If the man had been a vampire, he wouldn't have shown up on the camera. Whatever he is, he showed up crystal clear, even if glowing a little.

"Hmm. Okay, so maybe this is a stray dark master hitching a ride on a living person. Until a better idea comes along, it'll have to be my working theory. Can you tell me why everyone at the donut shop seemed to have the whole event removed from their memory? Even Sherbet forgot I'd asked him to run the plates on the van. Even a note he wrote for himself turned blank."

"Ah, the Rite of Unknowing," says Akhenaten. "It is a magical ritual that infiltrates the fabric of reality, focused on a particular event rather than person, unwinding it from mass consciousness."

I blink. "Umm. So if someone targeted Zandra's abduction with this rite, anyone who witnessed or heard about it would forget it ever happened?"

"It is one possibility," says Sebastian, his face brightening, his normal voice returning.

"Though I wonder how you have retained your memory of it, if so."

"Just special I guess." I shrug. "Might have something to do with me not being human or having a dark master. Or maybe it's not exactly the rite he mentioned."

"Possibly, yes."

"Ugh." I stare at the ceiling. "What the heck is going on?"

The swordsman raises an eyebrow. "Something fun, I hope."

Not the word I'd use to describe it, but I smile anyway. "Say, I don't suppose either of you have heard much of what you-know-who is doing?"

Sebastian chuckles. "Oh, come now, Samantha. You can say Elizabeth. She's not... what's his name from those novels. *Bal D'morte*?"

"Voldemort. Yeah, true. Suppose it's overly superstitious of me to avoid talking about her openly." I finish my last sip of wine and set the empty glass on the table. "I'm also guessing here. Between the release of magic and the escape of her loyalists from the Void, any supernatural goings on that no one seems to understand make me think she's responsible somehow."

"I'm afraid we haven't heard anything unusual," says Sebastian, a faint hint of 'why would I care what she does' in his voice.

True, his dark master is much older than her and regards Elizabeth as being beneath him… as well as a lunatic. Of course, Akhenaten also tends to consider women in general to be lessers. When I'd first brought her up, he'd commented about it having been a mistake to ever let women learn 'the art.' By that, I assume he means magic—not witchcraft, but the darker practices of blood rites and demonic alliances. Basically, the stuff dark masters use to become what they are. I told Zayn his dad was a product of his time, but this guy (Akhenaten, I mean) is way worse. He's more a product of a bygone *age* than 'his time.' Granted, he doesn't dislike women, more like a patronizing condescension. Not worth trying to convince him otherwise. Still infuriating, but some battles are pointless.

Obviously, Sebastian lived in a time when society had treated women much differently than today, but he's not as stuck in old ways of thinking as his dark master. He had likely once been quite the chauvinist, but he's mellowed out a great deal.

"Thank you again for the workout. See you next week."

"*Au revoir.*" He stands.

I get to my feet as well. We bow to each other… and I teleport home.

Chapter Fifteen
Too Forgettable

A two-hour sword training session has an inevitable consequence.

I need a shower, unlike Sebastian who is as dead as disco music. Guess I always tried my damndest to cling to life, or maybe a vampire's ability to sweat operated on a conscious basis, like activating features on a highly elaborate doll. Squeeze here to make her cry. Poke this button and you have to change her diaper, and so on. Some girl I went to grade school with had a doll that would 'pee.' As long as I live, I'll never understand how anyone thought diaper wetting was a good idea for a toy.

The instant my toes hit the bathmat after I

finish showering, the phone rings.

Tammy's the only other person in the house at the moment, so no big deal doing a hasty run to my bedroom with only a towel on. If not for being in the middle of the Zandra case, I'd have let it ring and called them back. The Caller ID shows Fullerton PD, which I assume to be a call from Detective Sherbet.

I swipe to answer and lean my head to the side, trying not to get the phone covered in wet hair. "Hello?"

"Sam?" asks Sherbet. "There's something really weird going on."

"Statement of the year."

He chuckles. "Seriously. Um… you asked me about something. I have a note here reminding me to call you regarding what I found, but I don't remember anything about the case."

"Argh." I bounce in frustration. "Yeah, something weird is going on. I asked you to try to find out who a black Mercedes van belongs to. Only got the first four of the plate. 78GX or 7BGX."

"Yes!" He hammers a fist onto his desk. "Now I remember! Dammit. It's not like me to forget. Must be getting old."

I put the phone on speaker and proceed to dry off. "It's not you. There's something else at work here. I've interviewed a ton of people about this and no one remembers a damn thing."

"What, like magic?"

"Definitely magic."

"You know I don't believe in the hocus pocus stuff."

"And you didn't used to believe in creatures that go slurp in the night, either. Unless you've got a better theory, the best answer I've gotten so far is some kind of spell. Whoever abducted Zandra must have done something mystical to cover their tracks. Everyone involved has holes in their memory. Even you, who I merely asked about the van."

"You're starting to freak me out here, Sam." He whistles. "You really believe in this stuff?"

"Think about who you're talking to and reconsider the question."

He chuckles. "Ehh… good point."

"So, did you run the plate?"

"I did. Then I called over to Corona PD, asked for the detective working the missing person case for Zandra Adams. They transfer me over to a Detective Weathersby, but she acted like they sent me to the wrong detective. Didn't have any recollection of being assigned the case."

Wow. Something *really* doesn't want this woman found. I really hope this isn't Elizabeth or she's become astonishingly powerful. Fingers crossed Dolores the psychic was right and I'm going to eventually find Zandra.

"Holy hell," says Sherbet suddenly.

"What now?"

"I thought I wrote down Detective Wentworth's number right here."

"You mean Weathersby."

"What did I say?"

"Wentworth."

"This weird shit of yours isn't only erasing memories, it's erasing ink, too. My notepad is blank."

"This is getting out of control," I mutter.

He types for a moment. "What the hell? Bah. I shouldn't be surprised."

"Surprised? At what?" I drop the towel and grab fresh clothes.

Sherbet grumbles. "The system keeps an activity log of who ran what searches. As far as I know, it's impossible to alter the log, at least not without being a major egghead. Anyway, there's no entry here showing me running this search. But I know I did... well, I think I did."

"Yeah, this is well beyond memory tampering."

"Oh, hey… didn't you say this woman's a screenwriter?"

"Yeah."

Four loud key presses echo over the line. Sherbet's a one-finger typist. "Rumor going around this morning about Quentin Arnbury. His wife reported him missing."

"Sounds like I should know that name, but I can't place it."

"Wow. Even I know this one, Sam. You ever hear of *Contest of Sovereignty*?"

"Oh, right… that medieval miniseries where like everyone dies. My kids love it."

Sherbet chuckles. "Not *all* the characters die, but yeah. That's the one. Arnbury's the guy who wrote the novels."

"No way. What happened?"

"Not my case. I'm homicide. Besides, it's up in Brentwood. Everyone worried the guy would drop dead before he finished the novel series, but I guess he pulled through. Couple of the guys here think he wanted a break from fame, so might've run off with a mistress."

"Mistress? Where'd that come from?"

Sherbet laughs. "Why would a guy fake a disappearance and not bring his wife?"

"Good point."

I pull my shirt on and fluff my hair out from

under it—and pause in mid-fluff.

Two missing writers. Well, one missing writer and one missing writer/director. Still, both creators in their own right. Were they Vincent Van Gogh, Charlie Reed and J.K. Rowling level creators? I didn't know, but I wasn't gonna go there out loud with Sherbet. What little I've shared with him about vampires has already pushed him to the edge of his ability to cope.

"Aha. Got something here but you're not going to like it."

I wrap my hair in the towel. "How bad?"

"There are no registrations in the system for a black Mercedes van starting with 78GX or 7BGX. My guess is you saw a fake plate, or the record vanished from the system the same way everything else about this seems to be deleting itself."

"Right..." I tap my foot. Seems the mundane world of police and computers is going to have to sit this one out. "Let me know if the people looking into Quentin Arnbury's disappearance have similar memory problems."

Sherbet chuckles. "Sure—if I remember."

I hang my head. What the hell am I going to tell Greta Adams about her mother?

"Thanks," I say.

"Anytime, Sam."

After I get off the phone, I go check on Tammy. She's curled up in bed, but not asleep.

"Hey, Tam Tam. How are you feeling?"

"Like I got hit by a truck," she rasps.

"It's almost dinner time. You hungry?"

She emits a weird noise. "Is it possible to be hungry and nauseated simultaneously?"

"Yeah. If you had the flu, I'd say have soup, but you're hungover. Once you start eating, you'll feel better."

"'Kay." She pushes herself up to sit. "Mom?"

"Yeah?"

"I'm not gonna drink that much ever again. Don't remember what happened at the party at all, and I feel like crap. Ugh. Why do people drink? There's nothing good about it."

I smile. "You overdid it. It's not so bad when you don't go too far. I know I promised not to get on you for it, so I won't, but I will say please be careful. Especially after you're in college. A girl getting drunk at a house party is…"

"Yeah, I know. At first, I didn't think any of the guys at Petey's would do anything… but they started giving me creepy looks."

"They'll probably behave themselves when they're sober. People do dumb things when they're drunk."

She looks down. "Are we gonna get in trouble?"

"Not from me. Looks like you're being punished enough already."

"I mean with the cops." She drags herself off the bed and stands on wobbly legs.

"Did you or your friends have anything to do with supplying the alcohol?"

She starts to shake her head, but nearly loses her balance from it. "No. We got there kinda late 'cause of Veronica's mall job. Everyone was already drunk by the time we walked in."

"Sounds like no one will remember who was there. So you should be fine."

Tammy wobbles over and grabs the doorjamb for balance. "Will you do me one little favor, Ma?"

I raise an eyebrow. "Depends on what it is."

"If anyone figures out my mother's the one who called the cops, will you make everyone forget it?"

"Heh. We'll see. Except for a couple guys out in the yard, everyone there was unconscious."

"Sorry." Tammy stares at the floor. "It got way out of control. Thanks for getting us out of there."

"Probably not what most parents would have done, but most parents haven't traveled back in time like a hundred million years. Slight shift in perspective of what's a serious problem."

She starts to laugh, but stops, wincing. "Ow."

"Headache?"

"Yeah."

I lead her out into the hall. "C'mon. Eat something, then take another Advil."

At least my daughter's headache is one a pill can help.

My headache is more metaphorical.

Chapter Sixteen
Familiar Pattern

Despite being a vampire, I have—for the most part—tried to play by the rules.

Meaning, I don't really like flaunting my supernatural abilities unless circumstances leave me no other choice. Ignoring trivial details like ethics, the law, and police might be normal for some supernatural creatures, but I've never felt the need to operate above mortal society—until now.

In much the same way no one bats an eye if a cop breaks the speed limit in the midst of pursuing a criminal, I justify taking my investigation to the next level. If Elizabeth, or some other powerful entity, is up to something, it will serve no one's best interest for me to handicap myself.

So, Sunday morning, I visited the Brentwood police station and helped myself to several brains. It didn't surprise me no one there had any memory of receiving a report from Quentin Arnbury's wife. There wouldn't be any police investigation into his disappearance. I didn't bother reminding anyone of it since it would be pointless as the cops would probably forget again within minutes of being reminded. Whatever happened to him isn't anything mortals are going to be able to help with, anyway. I know that now.

In the police station lobby, I look the guy up on my phone, since I didn't really know much about him other than his name. He's younger than I expected, only forty-four. His 'official' picture makes him look like he should be teaching high school English somewhere for advanced students... the 'cool' English teacher who'd sometimes come in to school wearing a medieval cloak or some such thing.

Visiting the police station didn't help much beyond giving me his home address, which isn't public information. Again, wild breach of ethics, but the situation has escalated beyond petty things like mortal laws.

I fly from the police station to Brentwood Heights, where Quentin Arnbury lives in a surprisingly ordinary house. It's nice—probably worth five times what mine is—but doesn't look like the sort of place the man responsible for a massively popular miniseries and novel series would live in. Guess Hollywood doesn't pay what it used to, or maybe the guy's like me. No need to show off the money. How much house does a person really need? I still can't wrap my brain around having a bank account so large. Here's hoping I stay true to myself and don't let the cash change me.

A woman I assume to be his wife answers the door. Her eyes are red around the edges and she has the look of little sleep to her.

"Mrs. Arnbury?" I ask.

"Yes. Who are you?"

"My name is Samantha Moon. I was in the middle of investigating a missing person case when I became aware that your husband has also disappeared. Do you have a few minutes to talk? I believe the cases might be related."

"Are you a detective?"

I poke her in the brain enough not to care about my answer. "I'm not affiliated with the police department. My investigation is from a different agency."

"Oh. Well, all right. Please, call me Patricia. Come in." She backs up so I can enter, closes the door, and leads me through a living room decorated with fantasy swords, paintings of dragons, and statues of elves to a giant kitchen decorated in slate grey with an island counter.

Okay, maybe I'm a little jealous. I've always wanted an island counter. My kitchen is kinda small.

"Thank you. What can you tell me about Quentin's disappearance?"

She sits at the table. "It didn't seem at first like anything unusual was going on. A car service showed up to give him a ride to a meeting with some executives from a movie studio. I didn't remember him having any such meeting, but Quentin did. He went with them and hasn't been back."

"How long ago was this?"

"Two days." She squeezes her hands into fists. "He's not answering his phone."

"Did you get a look at the car service driver or the car?"

"Yes." She looks at me. "They had one of those vans, kind of like some services use to take groups to the airport. There were two men. The tall one looked Middle Eastern. The other was short, with real wide shoulders. Looked like he could've lifted the whole van."

"Anything seem strange about the Middle Eastern guy?"

"He made me uncomfortable," says Patricia.

I peek at her thoughts. Amazingly, she does remember seeing them—and the van. The Middle Eastern guy is the same one from the security video at the Dunkin, only in her memory, he does not have a shimmery aura. He's smiling and apparently friendly, though she has an instinctual avoidance reaction to him. From what I gather, his very presence frightens her the same way mice shy away from cats. She can't articulate in words why she felt afraid of him, just did. The closest parallel I can think of is how people sometimes sense when they're in the same room as a serial killer and want to get the heck away as fast as possible.

OMG, Mom! Tammy squeaks in my head. *Are you seriously in Quentin Arnbury's house!?*

Yeah, I'm—

Crap! He's missing? Dammit, Mom, you gotta find him!

Trying to…

He's supposed to be working on a prequel series about the main character from the first book who dies at the end in a big twist.

Great, my daughter is fangirling. I'm working, Tammy.

Oops, sorry.

I refocus my thoughts at the broken woman in front of me. "You've had no contact at all from him or anyone making any sort of ransom demand?"

Patricia shakes her head. "No. Not a word. Do you have any leads yet?"

"Nothing concrete, but I have some suspicions."

I spend a little while trying to reassure her that 'we are doing everything we can to find him' and asking the usual questions about enemies, angry exchanges, dangerous fans, and so on. He gets tons of furious fan mail from people whose favorite characters die, but none of them reached a point where he or Patricia genuinely worried.

"I do tell him sometimes he kills off too many." She dabs her eyes with a napkin. "I think it takes away the emotional depth when he's got a dozen characters or more per book being killed off. He does it so much it's amazing people expect any character to last more than twenty pages. But, you know how people are. They get their favorite character and think *that's* the one he won't kill... then they're shocked when it happens."

"So I hear."

She looks up with a hint of a smile. "Not a fan?"

"My kids adore the show. I've seen a few episodes, but I get too invested in characters. As long as I don't watch the rest of the series, I can pretend the ones I like are still alive."

Patricia chuckles sadly. "Yes, Quentin sure loves his drama, doesn't he?"

"I'm going to do everything possible to find him." I glance around, tapping my foot. "I was wondering if you might be able to let me borrow something personal of his."

"Personal?" She raises an eyebrow.

"This is an unusual case. An object of emotional significance to him might help me figure out where he is. It doesn't have to be of physical value."

"Aren't you with the, umm... FBI or something? What you're asking sounds like something out of one of Quentin's stories."

"Ever watch *X-Files?* This case is something like one of those." I lean on her mentally, eroding her hesitation and suspicion I'm trying to take a souvenir.

"Hmm. Well... One moment." Patricia wanders off into the house.

I stand there feeling a little guilty, but honestly, this isn't stealing. Unless something goes *wildly* wrong, whatever item she lets me borrow is definitely coming back.

Tammy goes nuts in my head, rambling about characters from the series, wanting me to ask Patricia questions about why they did X or why Quentin made Y happen to them. I mentally raise my hands at her in a 'whoa, slow down' gesture. As in, let me find the guy first—if I can—before we pester her about stuff. Her husband is missing.

Oh. Duh. Sorry.

Still working, hon.

Sorry again.

Patricia returns carrying an old-looking orangey-brown inter-office envelope with a string tie closure. "This is a story he wrote when he was in high school. His teacher loved it. Because of that man's response, Quentin decided to pursue being an author."

Oh, wow. Eek. I'm going to feel horrible if anything happens to this. Not to mention, the first real story written by the man responsible for *Contest of Sovereignty* might draw a ridiculous bid on one of those celebrity memorabilia sites, but if it ever ends up there, it won't be my doing.

"Wow... thank you for entrusting me with

this. I'll get it back to you as soon as humanly possible."

She twitches, a clear sign her actual desire is at war with my compulsion. "Care for some tea?"

"Thank you, but I've already taken up more than enough of your time."

Patricia leans on the counter, her expression once again sad. "All right. Will you please call me if you find anything?"

"Of course."

We trade phone numbers.

When I go back through the living room full of fantasy stuff, Tammy squees in my head and starts rambling about how she can't believe I'm in this guy's house. Before Patricia can open the front door, I insert a memory of seeing me walk outside and get in a grey 'FBI style' sedan. While she's standing there stuck in the bewildered fog of a vampiric mental alteration, I teleport home, specifically to my office.

It's kinda strange to me that whatever 'spell' is erasing memories, computer files, and even handwritten Post-It notes didn't affect Patricia. I wonder if it's because she's too close to Quentin for it to work? According to the stuff Allison has been teaching me, magic is super sensitive to things like true names, family lines, blood relations, and so on. Someone who wouldn't recognize Quentin or Zandra from anyone else on the street has zero defense against magical tampering to remove memory of them. Close family or friends—like a wife—would be protected from casual magical alteration. Even for me, making someone forget a spouse, parent, or child is so difficult it's technically impossible. A vampire could make someone temporarily forget someone close to them, but the implant would invariably crumble in hours, days, or weeks depending on the strength of their connection.

Quentin Arnbury is responsible for one of the most successful fantasy television shows ever. He's got a crapload of fans. Damn good chance this guy is a creator. Zandra's not as big a name, but still has many loyal fans. She, too, might be a creator. It might explain how a B-list director/screenwriter has such a rabid following. Both of them being creators is the only possible reason I can think of for Elizabeth—or Mr. Middle Eastern vampire enigma—to be interested in them.

Okay, so figuring out magic is involved doesn't tell me anything new.

But I think I'm going to need to *use* magic to get anywhere on this case. My witchy powers might have come back, but they're not exactly the stuff of legends. Time for me to put some of my HUD training to work. Not the sort of thing one expects to reference in terms of paranormal oddities, but I did learn one thing working for the federal government.

Delegation.

Chapter Seventeen
Gloves Off

I leave Quentin's high school creative writing project on my desk and teleport to Zandra's house.

Yes, this is straight up breaking and entering plus robbery, but I'm only borrowing... something. After a while of looking around for an item of seeming emotional significance, I settle on an object from her writing desk. I can't really tell what it's supposed to be. Maybe a paperweight. Maybe an ash tray. Maybe a coaster. Whatever it is, it's rather obviously made by a small child—assuming Greta from years ago—as evidenced by the questionable craftsmanship and the 'MOM' painted on it under a giant heart.

Zandra has to feel something for this object. It's certainly not on her desk for any practical purpose. Ill-gotten gains in hand, I teleport home.

Time to cheat and take the gloves off, as Jacky would say.

I call Allison.

"Nothing yet," she says by way of answering.

"You remember?"

"Of course. I'm not senile yet."

"Not that. Something is making other people forget. For some reason, it's not working on me." I explain Sherbet forgetting to run the plate and also his Post-It note going blank, plus the Dunkin employees all entirely forgetting Zandra ever went there, as well as the Brentwood Police Department entirely losing any sense Quentin Arnbury went missing.

"Whoa, this is big." She whistles. "What are you thinking is going on?"

"How would you react to me saying I keep thinking about Elizabeth here?"

"I'd say you're having a witch's hunch."

"Is that a thing?"

She laughs. "When things just come out of nowhere, and keep doing it, you're picking up on vibes."

"Oh, great. Vibes. This is going to end with us sitting naked around a fire out in the woods sipping matcha tea and huffing incense, isn't it?"

"Only if you want it to."

I laugh. "Not really. I've been picking up on such vibes, truth be known. Had one last month about Danny."

"What about Danny?"

"I'm pretty sure he will be leaving my son soon."

"Interesting. Does Anthony know?"

"No. Not yet. I figure I would cross that bridge if and when Danny does leave."

"Good strategy. No reason to upset your son now. So what's up?"

I collect myself, shrugging off a pang of sadness and regret over my lost marriage. "I collected some emotionally significant items for both missing people. Will you help me do the crystal ball thing?"

"Scrying? Sure. I'll be over in an hour."

"Want me to teleport you?"

"Naw, I'll drive. I need to think about the spell a little."

"Sounds good. See you soon."

Allison arrives just as Tammy finishes reading Quentin Arnbury's high school story. She called it 'weird.' Apparently, it's about a guy whose coffee cup contains a demon that talks him into doing various odd things. Nothing whatsoever to do with the show she loves or even sword & sorcery in general.

We set up in the dining room, Allison having brought a giant bag of divination supplies. Mostly candles, incense, some crystals, tea leaves just in case, and several jars of powdered herbs and esoteric stuff like bat wing powder.

"So, the ghosts haven't been very talkative about this whole thing," says Allison while smoothing out the pentacle cloth—a black tablecloth into which she embroidered a silver pentacle. "Other than telling me Zandra's not dead."

"That's a plus."

Tammy stands at the end of the table, arms folded, her black hair half covering her face. She's wearing a band T-shirt for 'Unleash the Archers' with jeans, toenails and fingernails painted black like her lipstick.

Allie's gone completely mainstream. Beige sweater, dark blue skirt. She totally looks like a grade school teacher.

My daughter bursts out laughing. Allison smirks at me.

Ack. Both of them can see into my head.

"No offense," I say to Allie.

"None taken. I like the new me."

I pick up on her thoughts, and realize she's 'toning it down' because of Anthony. At some point during our European vacation, my son developed a legit crush on her. No surprise there. Allison's a personal trainer on the side in Beverly Hills, and a decade ago had been a stripper. That's more than enough to make any teenage boy lose his mind.

"He's a sweet boy, but best to keep things under wraps, don't you agree?" she says.

"I agree."

"Okay, let's do this." Allison takes a seat, positioned at the middle of the rectangular table's longer side. She pulls a black cloth off her crystal ball. Yeah, she's got one. And yes, we already made the 'it takes balls to be a witch' joke about a million times.

I sit opposite her and put the envelope containing the story plus the unidentifiable object in the middle of the pentacle.

Tammy remains standing at the end as a curious spectator. "What the heck is that thing?"

"Beats me," I mutter. "Her kid made it for her and it was on her desk, so I figured it has some emotional weight."

After she lights the candles, Allison and I clasp hands over the two items. I do my best to contribute whatever witchy power I have to my friend's ability to scry. She closes her eyes, concentrating on her desire to receive information from the universe around us. Soon, she bites her lip, fidgets, then rests her hands on the envelope.

Several minutes later, she picks up and manipulates the child's art project like a blind person 'seeing' it with their hands.

"Cold…" says Allison. "People tied to these objects are feeling cold. There's confusion, too."

Yeah, no kidding.

Tammy covers her mouth to hold in the snicker at my thought.

"Distance. Far away," whispers Allison before growling, her face scrunching up as if she's fighting off a bout of brain freeze.

She abruptly lurches forward like an invisible force grabbed her by the hair, intent on bouncing her head off the table. I thrust my hands out fast enough to catch her forehead before her nose smashes into the unidentifiable object. She hits my hand with enough force it sounds like I slapped her.

"Ow," mutters Allison in a toneless voice.

"Whoa." Tammy races over and holds the back of her head in both hands. "Something yanked her hair."

"I'm getting magical feedback," says Allison in a trancelike voice. "Something's blocking me."

Tammy runs to grab a pillow off the couch and puts it on the table where Allison's face would make contact if the same attack repeats.

Allison opens her eyes. "Gah. That sucked. I've got a red print on my forehead from smacking into your hands so hard, don't I?"

I make a pinchy gesture. "Just a minor red mark."

She huffs, blowing her bangs up. "I only received a vague sense of coldness and confusion."

"Hmm." I eye the bag of supplies she brought. "Not much to go on. You said something about distance, too. Anything else you can try?"

"Possibly." Allison goes for the crystal ball next.

"And what about your distant viewing?" I ask. Allison can 'see' with the best of them, which made her work at the psychic hotline so effective... and also her work on her late night radio show.

She shakes her head. "First thing I tried to do. Blocked. I need magic to break through."

Five minutes later, the ball turns jet black. A red glow starts deep within, rapidly expanding until the crystal is like a window into a fiery inferno. Amid a blast of heat, a flaming human skull with eight-inch horns launches into the air and starts flying around the room, emitting an ear-piercing shriek.

Allison jumps out of her chair, emitting a startled yelp, raising her hand toward the freakish thing.

Tammy stares with a 'WTF' expression.

The skull swerves around and flies straight at us, spitting a tiny fireball at Allison. She whips her left hand up as well, creating a tiny disc of blue light to block the magical projectile. I obey my first instinct and yank the Devil Killer out of its pocket dimension straight into a thrust at the passing skull.

My blade cracks through the bone and comes out the top of the cranium. Fire belches out the hole where the sword pierced. Despite being impaled, the creature keeps trying to fly, but isn't strong enough to move me. While I hold the thing still like a marshmallow over a campfire, Allison blasts it with an energy bolt.

It bursts into a cloud of smoke.

"What the fff—udge was that?" I whisper.

Tammy looks around.

I glance at her. "Think there's more?"

"No, I'm looking around for the little kid who can't hear bad words."

"Hate to say it, but..." Allison emits a nervous laugh. "It looked like a pyre-scream."

"Yeah, it did." Tammy nods.

"Why do both of you know what a pyre-scream is and I don't?" I ask, sliding the sword back into its dimensional pocket.

Tammy points at me, shakes her head sadly. "She doesn't watch *Contest of Sovereignty*."

"Those things are supposed to be fictional." Allison brushes her fingers at the ashes on the table. "In the books, they're like these nuisance demons. Not particularly powerful, but when forty of them are trying to kill you, it's not pleasant."

Tammy whistles. "Yeah. There's a scene where Lady Emlys is in the depths of Loreholm and she's running over this narrow-ass bridge and a whole storm of pyre-screams come after her."

"Right, but this thing is from a book of fiction?" I look back and forth between them. "It's not supposed to exist."

Allison stares at me. "Unless he's a creator."

"The world of *Estaeron* actually exists somewhere?" Tammy goes wide-eyed.

I nod. "Considering we've just seen a real pyre-scream, if Quentin is a creator, then yes. Somewhere, a dimension exists exactly like his world."

"You wanna go there, don't you?" Allison grins eagerly.

"No way." Tammy shakes her head. "Are you crazy? I'd be dead in two episodes... err two days."

"Not if you kept your head down." Allison pokes at her.

"Still, that would be boring. The whole point of going there would be to see exciting stuff. And seeing exciting stuff will get me killed." Tammy gestures at me. "Besides. Our reality is plenty exciting already."

I take my daughter's hand. "Can you try to find them, sweetie?"

"I dunno, Mom. I'm really tuned into your head, which is how I can talk to you when you're far away. No idea how to find a specific person I've never met before."

Allison covers the crystal ball, pushes it aside, and relocates the old story and (possible) paper weight to the middle of the table. Oh, you know... it might be an attempt at a birdhouse.

Nah. "Maybe I can create a bridge for her to use. Tammy, hold hands with us and give me a few minutes to try something."

Since the dining room table is a big rectangle and Tammy doesn't want to stand and stretch to reach us, she climbs up and sits cross-legged on the table. Allison has an 'omg she looks like a younger Sam' thought, followed by 'ack! When did she stop being a child?' Tammy smirk-blushes at her while removing her faerie amulet and setting it beside her. She cringes at the inrush of chaotic voices, then reaches out to clasp our hands.

Alas, she needs to take the amulet off for long range telepathy. At least she's able to handle hundreds of voices all talking at once for short stints. It's honestly no worse than being in the cafeteria at a busy high school.

Magic wafts off Allison toward the story and ceramic mystery item, an active spell rather than passive scrying. No doubt reacting to Allie thinking 'okay, ready,' Tammy shuts her eyes and takes on this meditative expression. The posture she's sitting in only adds to her monk-like appearance. 'Sedate and calm' are two words I'd never use to describe my daughter.

"Stop making me smile," mutters Tammy.

I grin.

"You might feel a weak hint of someone's thoughts coming from these items. If my spell worked, they're going to act like a bridge to the person's actual mind. You should be able to follow it back and connect to them directly... if you can reach far enough."

"Okay," whispers Tammy.

Allison looks at me and thinks, *If they're magically protected, her psychic snooping directly into their heads will hopefully get around it. The magic's blocking distant seeing, but she's using telepathy.*

Here's hoping, I think back.

A few minutes later, Tammy squeezes my hand. "I'm seeing a tiny jet plane. Like one of those ones rich people use."

I picture a Leer jet. "This?"

"Umm. Yeah. It's flying over the ocean. The water's real dark. Oh, there's the shore. Land's coming. Snowy."

Allison lets go of our hands. She pulls a laptop out of her bag, flips it open.

Tammy sways side to side. "Still flying. Everything looks the same."

"Here." Allison turns the laptop to face us, Google Maps on the screen, and guides Tammy's hand onto the touchpad. "Show us where. Don't think about it. Let your finger move however it wants to."

My daughter taps the touchpad like she's petting a cat on the nose with one finger at first, then presses harder while making a face like someone said something really stupid. Or maybe she's concentrating. She swipes at the touchpad as if she can see the screen through her closed eyes, scrolling the map left and upward.

She zooms.

Then clicks on a dot.

The instant the map centers on a small city, Tammy's eyes snap open. "They're there."

We all look at the screen: Barrow, Alaska.

"Ouch," mutters Allison. "That's a bit of a ride. I don't think the Momvan's up for it."

I exhale. "Nope. She's most certainly not."

Chapter Eighteen
Varying Degrees of Cruelty

I can't believe we are planning a trip to Barrow, Alaska late on a Sunday afternoon.

It shouldn't really shock me after everything else weird in my life. Popping off on a whim to the coldest state in the country is fairly tame compared to 'oh, hey, vampires are real.' Allison thinks she should come with me. We go back and forth tossing up ideas as to how to handle this from a logistical perspective. Tammy busies herself on the laptop.

"It's 2,947 miles away in a straight line," says Tammy.

Talos flies faster than my angel wings, but even he can't compete with a jet aircraft. Carrying Allison for close to ten hours would suck in nice weather. Forget it in an area where the temps can drop into double digit negatives. Flying 250 miles an hour in negative thirty-degree weather would feel like negative a hundred. She'd need *serious* winter gear and still probably end up with deadly frostbite.

Not sure even Talos could handle those temperatures. His wing membranes could freeze and crack. Allison thinks it won't bother him because he's a dragon and dragons are magical fourth-dimensional creatures, so the laws of physics don't really apply to them.

I've never been anywhere with such frigid temperatures, says Talos in my head. *I am unsure what effect they would have on me. I am willing to attempt it.*

I can't ask you to do that.

If it is unworkable, I will return home and you can teleport back to a warm environment.

You do realize it would leave me standing there naked for the few seconds it takes me to teleport. What if I become disoriented in the extreme cold and can't concentrate enough to teleport?

Then I suspect you will be highly uncomfortable. It's not like you'll die.

Oh. Right. My new self is so much more human-like than before it's easy to forget I'm still a vampire. Still, if I freeze solid, my ass is going to be stuck out there until someone finds me. Allison mentions some frozen guy named Ötzi people found in a glacier in 1991. Yeah, no. I don't really want to end up scaring the ever-loving hell out of a bunch of scientists when they thaw me out and I sit up.

"In November, Barrow, Alaska—also known as Utqiagvik—is permanently dark," says Tammy, reading from the screen.

"Nice for ordinary vampires," I say. "Wonder if that's why they chose the spot."

"I dunno. Sunblock would freeze in the bottle for most of the year up there," says Allison.

"Good point."

"But for like three months out of the year, they get 24/7 darkness."

"So maybe they're seasonal vamps," I say. "Makes sense if you don't have kids in school."

Allison chuckles.

"Mom, why would Elizabeth kidnap creators?" asks Tammy.

My grin falters. So does Allison's. "You say that like you know something we don't."

My daughter nods. "Right before I snapped out of the link, Quentin Arnbury walked into a room and Elizabeth was standing right there, smiling at him." Tammy picks up her amulet and puts it back on, making an 'ahh, much better face.'

"Are you sure it was her?" I ask.

"Yeah. I saw her in your memory after you, umm… barfed her out." Tammy cringes. "By the way, that is in my top five of most disgusting things ever seen in someone's head."

"Eww." I wince. "I don't want to know what beats it."

Tammy holds up her hand, ticking items off by tapping fingers. "The way it felt when you got swallowed by a dragon. When the demon exploded and covered you with slime. Barfing up Elizabeth. This kid at school who has perverted fantasies about zombies—he's totally going to end up being a serial killer. And basically every time I look into Anthony's head without warning. Seriously. What is *wrong* with boys?"

I chuckle.

"Okay, knowing *she* is involved adds a new layer." Allison taps a finger to her chin. "We've been waiting for her to make a move. Should you call Max?"

"Possibly. He might be able to help out with the cold issue if nothing else."

"Gonna see if I can find anything else in Mr. Arnbury's head." Tammy pulls off her faerie amulet again.

I rest a hand on her shoulder. "Be careful."

"What's she doing?" Allison shifts her gaze back and forth between us.

"Quentin's thinking…" Tammy stares into space for a few minutes, then her eyes flutter as she breaks contact. "Whoa."

Allie and I stare expectantly at her.

"Sec." She puts the amulet back on and spends a moment rubbing her temples. "Still a bit hung over to concentrate. Trying not to throw up."

"Hungover?" Allie gives me a look.

"Yeah. Life lessons come in multiple forms," I say.

"Okay, this is super weird." Tammy picks at a fray of denim by her ankle. "So, Quentin is—wow, I can't believe I peeked into *his* mind." She exhales hard, fighting the urge to fangirl. "Umm, he's trying to make a world. I mean, Elizabeth is forcing him and some other creators to make an entirely new world for her."

Allison blinks. "Since when is she a patron of the arts?"

I pace around the narrow space between my chair and the bookshelf. Our 'dining room' is stuffed into an alcove behind the living room, not a whole lot of space. "Hmm. Creating an entirely new world? Maybe her plans to go upward in the dimensions didn't work out? She's powerful, but for all the BS coming out of her mouth, she's still not a higher-dimensional being."

"Yeah." Allison sets her hands on her hips. "I bet she's not as powerful as she brags about, or she'd already have been trying to conquer the world."

"Why conquer the world when she can make a new one?" asks Tammy. "She can have the creators write her in as a goddess in whatever world they make for her."

"Sounds like a lot less work than taking over this world." Allison shrugs. "Make a new one already the way you want it to be."

I shake my head. "It *can't* be that simple. Wouldn't she have done it already, if so? Besides, she wants to dominate this world out of revenge for being cast into the Void the first time. She always talked about what the world would be like when she finally put her plan into motion. Tried to bribe me into helping her by offering me power if I'd let her out of the box I kept her in."

"Could be lies," says Allison. "She had you convinced your destiny was to be the one to bear the great burden of keeping her contained, but she really set you on a course to kill the Red Rider."

Tammy raises her hand. "Can we invoke the 'he needed killing' defense?"

"Yes," I say, then sigh. "And Allie's right. I convinced myself the fate of the world sat on my shoulders. She exploited my pride and my drive to do the right thing. I swallowed the story whole."

"Point is..." Allison scratches her head. "Maybe taking over this world wasn't ever her goal. Or maybe she thought about it but changed her mind. An entirely new world custom-made for her wouldn't have you, me, an army of Light Warriors, and whatever else might stand in her way."

I nod. "A nuclear bomb is pretty much game over for any vampire or werewolf or Lichtenstein monster... probably game over for anything supernatural. We heal rapidly, but if we're reduced to a cloud of vapor, I don't think our extreme healing is gonna work."

"She'd cause a lot of pain and suffering before the military even got involved on that scale," says Allison. "They might have magical means of messing up technology or terrifying and controlling soldiers. If so, the military will eventually hit her with a missile from a drone.

Way high up, she'd never see it coming in time to cast a spell."

"And if she attacks out in the open," I say, "the entire world is going to become aware of magic, vampires, and everything else. It would probably set off riots. One world leader thinks it's the end times and they hit the button… no more Earth to even rule over."

"Quentin is definitely working on creating a new world, along with other creators." Tammy scoots off the table and hops down. "It took us five minutes to figure taking over this world would be too difficult or impossible for her. Elizabeth made her plans back in the freakin' Dark Ages, right? She never imagined anything like modern weapons. So, she has these creators make a world like Estaeron or Dur or Middle-Earth, where they don't have technology and magic is really strong."

"Sounds likely," says Allison. "Especially if they make the magic overpowered. She'd be a goddess. Elizabeth wants to be worshiped more than she wants to punish this world. Evil is usually lazy, right? Fastest, quickest path to power is the most appealing no matter who gets hurt."

Hmm. I tap my foot, thinking. "So do we even do anything? If she's going to leave our world and take all of her dark masters with her into some other place, she's basically doing my job for me, right?"

Allison stares at me. "How do you figure?"

"My 'job' here is to protect the world from Elizabeth destroying it, right?"

Tammy shakes her head. "Not really. She made you think fate and destiny chose you to stand between her and everyone's lives."

I fidget. My kid's got a point. Okay, I really did fall for Elizabeth's lie. Maybe I'm not the 'savior of the Earth' I spent the bulk of the past fourteen years thinking myself to be. "Possibly. The only real conflict I had with her—other than the woman being a complete evil bitch—is believing she wanted to conquer the world. If she's just going to leave on her own, is there a real reason for us to get in the way?"

"Yeah." Tammy nods. "Do you really think she's going to let the creators go home after they're done? She's probably going to kill them."

"She can't." I shake my head. "Unless the world they make for her develops a following so the public consciousness keeps it alive, killing the creators who made it destroys the entire world."

Allison winces. "Once they're done creating, Elizabeth might have them turned into vampires so they live forever, and keep them imprisoned as an anchor for her universe."

"We don't know that, but it's definitely something I'd want to prevent." I grumble to myself, still pacing. "Is it wrong for us to allow her to inhabit a new reality custom made for her? The people in that world would certainly face a cruel existence… but they wouldn't exist at all otherwise. Is preventing their coming into being worse than allowing them to exist in a state of perpetual misery?"

"Are they even real people or just characters?" asks Tammy. "Like NPCs in a video game."

"I'll pretend I know what you said." I chuckle.

"You know the game Ant's always playing? It's a fake world, right? And some of the 'people' he interacts with aren't real. Just computer programs. NPC means non-player character. They look like characters, but they're not being controlled by another player. Do creators have the power to make like legit souls, or would the world be full of cardboard cutouts who only speak a few scripted lines of dialogue?"

Allison and I exchange a 'who knows' glance.

"When I visited Dur, the people there

seemed as real as anyone else." I stop pacing. "No matter what happens, we have to get Zandra, Quentin, and whoever else they've abducted out of there safely."

Allison and Tammy both nod.

"Which means I have to go to Barrow, Alaska… somehow."

"*We* have to go," says Allison.

Tammy squirms. "I'm going to end up being dragged into this, aren't I?"

"Not if I can help it." I pat her on the shoulder. "Your most important job is staying safe. You guys sit tight for now. I'll be back soon."

"Where are you going?" asks Allison.

"To see Max."

I close my eyes and summon the dancing flame. The alchemist's library appears within a tiny keyhole-sized portal in the distance. At my urging, it rushes closer, expanding to the width of a doorway. I step through into colder air thick with the fragrance of incense.

"Hello, Sam," says Max. "I had a feeling I'd see you soon."

Chapter Nineteen
Your Mother is at it Again

"We have a problem," I say. "But I'm not sure how big it is."

"Oh?" He quirks an eyebrow. "My intuition told me we would meet. Shall I assume this is in regard to my mother?"

I nod. "Yeah. And oh, crap!"

"Hmm?"

"Just figured something out." I snap my fingers. "Elizabeth is behind the abduction of several creators. The guy with the weird shimmery aura. Akhenaten said he'd seen the guy before in the Void, but didn't know him. He *has* to be one of Elizabeth's followers who's managed to possess a still-living person."

"Yes, you mentioned the aura the other day on the phone." Max pauses.

"I'm sensing you're holding something back."

"Merely a worry of mine. I have no reason to suspect it has come to pass."

"Max…" I hold my arms out to either side. "We're in uncharted territory here. One of the things they told me during training is never to ignore a hunch. Don't take it as truth off the bat, but definitely look into whatever your gut wants to say."

He paces, his face cycling through various degrees of concern, dismissal, and dread. "I've been wondering as to the purpose for my mother's desire to go upward into dimensions. Even to beings like dark masters, the inherently unstable energies there can be dangerous. Her desire to be a goddess often pushes her to defy matters of personal safety in her quest for power. She'd think nothing of risking destruction for a chance at godlike powers."

"You're working toward an eventual theory here, right?" I smile.

He chuckles. "Yes. The higher up she goes, the greater the power her magical abilities have."

"Right. Dimensions are exponentially more

powerful, but she is still a third-dimensional being."

"True. However, she can tap the power of the fourth or fifth dimension. You saw it firsthand when she divested herself of you, generating a body of her own."

"Oh, shit…" I blink at him, not liking where he's going with this. "You think she might have found a way to do the same thing for other dark masters? Grow bodies for them?"

"It's a working theory. I've been unable to find any comparable being with a thin radiance of white light surrounding them."

"Akhenaten said it reminded him of how the dark masters appear in the void."

Max emits a long sigh, nodding. "Could be, my mother has manipulated the forces of the higher dimension to allow her followers to manifest in a physical form."

"So what are they? Vampires?"

"More or less… though they might not be vulnerable to sunlight. Also, their power would not be reduced by the need to gradually acclimate to a mortal host."

"So, basically total badasses?" I cringe.

He holds a hand up in a 'wait' gesture. "This is why I hadn't said anything yet. No need to panic. What we're talking about is not proven.

We're only guessing."

"Humor me just in case?"

Max purses his lips in thought. "This would be a powerful individual, a dark master unlimited by the weakness of being trapped inside someone else's body. It takes many centuries for a new host to acclimate to the master within."

"That's why vampires start off fairly weak and get more powerful with time," I say.

"Correct. And they still seldom reach the full power the master is capable of. If these... physically embodied dark masters now reside in a corporeal form all their own, it would make very dangerous adversaries of them."

I bite my lip. "How bad are we talking here?"

"It would depend on the individual, but basically someone with great magical abilities plus the physical strength, speed, and powers of the oldest vampires."

"Oof."

"Dangerous but not impossible to defeat, especially for you."

"Me?" I can't help but blink.

"You are closer to them than you realize. A being of singular essence. Not a dark master trapped inside a limiting body. I take liberties here, but you are close to a light master if such a thing existed."

"Does it?"

"Not as far as I know." He chuckles. "What I'm saying is, these... eh, *ascendant* masters would be singular beings. No human frailty or second consciousness limiting them. It is the same with you. Azrael and Poendraz both contributed to your strength. And let's not forget what the Red Rider's cataclysmic release of energy did."

"Poendraz only gave me a little flight speed boost, and it doesn't work on Earth." I shrug. "And my witchcraft is still pretty anemic."

"You are channeling it in different ways than energy bolts. Speed, strength, toughness. Haven't you wondered how you've managed to hit Sebastian at all despite the vast difference in your age?"

"Figured he's holding back for training purposes."

Max smiles. "He would never *let* you hit him. Not only is he too prideful, Akhenaten would want him to dissuade a woman from learning how to fight with a blade by making you feel so inept and hopeless you gave up."

"Oh, hmm." I'd ask how Max knows Sebastian's dark master so well, but studying them is kind of his life's work. Not to mention, Max is likely the second most powerful telepath I know. Undoubtedly, he's watching my swordplay in my memory even now.

He smiles. "Undoubtedly."

"So, you're telling me I can take these guys on?"

"If they exist."

"Got any better ideas for what I saw on the security video? Would a dark master possessing a living human be able to mind-control anyone?"

"Doubtful."

"Okay, so new working theory—Elizabeth is somehow able to give her people physical bodies. Do you think I can take them on?"

"Yes, but they won't be easy. Those zombies in Denmark? Make them smart and give them magic."

"Lovely." I exhale hard. If not for those creators' lives in the balance, it would be damn tempting to simply let Elizabeth leave this world to her own private dimension and forget she ever existed. "I have other problems. I need to get to Barrow, Alaska as fast as possible and deal with the cold. Any suggestions?"

He grins. "As a matter of fact, I have an amulet ready for you."

"You just happen to have it?" He smiles. "While you wear it, you will be unaffected by extremes of normal temperature."

I blink. "That doesn't make sense. What's an 'extreme of normal'?"

"It makes perfect sense." He winks.

"Maybe to an alchemist."

He waves for me to follow and leads me around behind his counter, through a red curtain, and into the back room. "Simple, really. The ambient temperature of any natural place on Earth will not affect you, regardless of how severe. Anywhere from Antarctica to Death Valley, you will feel comfortable even if under or overdressed. However, if you jump in fire, you will still burn."

"Oh. So any normal temperature not harmful to the body is fine. What about frostbite?"

"Only if you encounter the cold equivalent of fire... liquid nitrogen."

"Got it. Only super extremes of temperature."

"Here you are, Sam." Max hands me a pendant about the size of a quarter on a thin chain. One side bears a bas-relief of a snowflake, the other a stylized sun. "While wearing this, you will suffer no discomfort from cold or heat."

"How did you know I would need something like this, Max?"

"Message from Azrael."

"Seriously? You'd think he could've slipped me a note about Alaska and saved me running around in circles for a week."

"I assume the message came from him. It is the most logical explanation." Max pulls out a cell phone.

"He sent you a text?"

Laughing, Max shakes his head. "No, I am about to call my associate to prepare the jet for me and my fellow Light Warriors."

"You have a private jet?"

"I do. One does not live thousands of years and not save a few bucks. This will be faster than your dragon friend. If my mother's plan is set in motion, we will need to mobilize. The Light Warriors have been preparing for this moment for centuries. It will take a little time for us to gather our forces."

"We don't have time. She's assembled a bunch of creators. I've gotta get them out of there... or at least put myself between her and them to buy your people time. I have to get there as fast as possible. Talos is going to take roughly ten hours to get up there. How long until you're ready to go?"

He bows his head. "Between prep and flight

time, roughly the same. Perhaps slightly faster in favor of Talos. It might be better for you to take the lead. Mother may have agents watching us. They would certainly become aware of my jet heading straight toward them."

"Damn. Okay. I'll go right now. Feels like I need more time to prepare, but no idea what I'd even do *to* prepare."

"Sam…" Max rests his hands on my shoulders. "You've been preparing for this showdown ever since the night you went for a jog in Hillcrest Park."

"Why am I so nervous then?"

"Because if you make a misstep, trying to take on multiple ascendant dark masters at once, possibly my mother as well, could very well lead to your final destruction."

I swallow. "Oh, so no pressure."

Chapter Twenty
Cold Pizza

Talos saves me from a mire of overthinking —and a long, tedious flight.

He reminded me I teleported to Azrael's palace a while ago, and it had been my first time there. Not sure how I got caught up thinking teleportation wasn't an option. All I had to focus on for the palace had been an illustration in Max's book. Google Earth should be as good or better than a drawing, right? Besides, hadn't I teleported to Mars based on a Rover picture? I had, of course. Actually, I did know what had happened. That damn forgetting spell must've gotten to me, too. Or maybe I'm not thinking straight due to anxiety. Luckily, I have Talos to remind me.

While Max rushes off to mobilize his allies, I teleport home.

Allison launches from the sofa and runs over. "Sam! Something weird is going on."

"No kidding." I exhale. "You still have Barrow up on Google? I'm going to try teleporting."

"Yeah, but..." Allison pulls on my arm. "Millicent told me not to go. Tammy, too. She didn't say why, but sounded scared."

Uh oh. Not a good sign at all. "Did she say anything about *me* going there?"

Allison shakes her head. "No, just that it's a real bad idea for Tammy and me."

"All right. I'd rather you guys stay out of harm's way if at all possible anyway." I walk over to the dining room table and spin the laptop around to look at the screen.

"So what's your plan?" asks Allison.

"Max is rallying the troops, but it's going to take him and his people several hours to get there. I'm going to go in and try to get the creators out unhurt. Not planning on a confrontation." Google doesn't have a street view for the place, only some random photos. I click on one that puts me in front of a little blue shack. A sign above the door says 'East Coast Pizzeria.'

Seems the owner is somewhat confused where they are.

"But, Sam..." Allison hovers over my shoulder, looking at the screen. "Do you have any idea where to even go once you're there? Elizabeth is going to sense you."

"Yeah. So she will. What are you suggesting? Not like she's going to take off running if she's deep into her world-building project."

"*You* might not want a confrontation, but *she* will start one." Allison pokes me in the shoulder. "Millicent didn't necessarily say we shouldn't go with you to Barrow... only to wherever Elizabeth is."

"Which could be one and the same place." I fold my arms. "I'm not going to ignore Millicent's warning and put my kid—or you—in harm's way."

"But if you go alone, Elizabeth is definitely going to sense you and she might kill the people she's kidnapped. Or come after you. Tammy can conceal our presence but not from 3,000 miles away. We've already worked it out."

"Oh you have, have you?" I sigh. "What are you talking about?"

"Anthony's on his way here now. We'll stay in Barrow"—she points at the screen—"probably in that pizza place. The Fire Warrior can take care of any threats there, but he's probably going to end up killing more pizza than anything."

I chuckle despite my nerves.

Allison puffs hair off her face. "We tried to get Kingsley to come with us, but he's in court right now. The judge won't excuse him for 'fighting evil across dimensions.' Go figure."

I sigh, but before I can say anything else, Anthony hurries in the front door with Tammy behind him. My son has a 'let's do this' expression. I'm not the only one in this family who's been living in fear (maybe fear's a bit too strong a word, more like constant nagging dread) of what Elizabeth is going to do at any moment. Ant sure seems to be eager to finally face the 'thing' we've been anxious about happening for so many years.

As if it's going to be easy or even over. We have two reasonable options here: beat her, or die trying. Even if we do defeat her, she's not going to stop. Max and the Light Warriors already defeated her once and only sent her to the Void. If we manage to win, we'd only be buying more time dreading her next move.

It beats dying, so, yeah. We go.

"Ma..." Anthony hurries over. "Tam's already explained everything. Are you sure we're only going to sit around doing nothing at a, what, pizza place? Not sure you should go alone. Millicent didn't say anything about *me* going with you being bad."

"Oh, heck no. You're not even sixteen yet, kiddo."

Allison makes a face at me like 'he's bigger than some grown men.'

"February, Ma."

"February is still three months away."

"*March* is three months away. You're getting semantic with weeks here." He stares pleadingly at me.

"Since when do you use words like semantic?" asks Tammy. "Did you stop sleeping through English class?"

"Excuse me one second." Anthony walks over to the couch, picks up a pillow, and hurls it at Tammy, hitting her in the face.

"Ack!" Tammy flails her arms to keep her balance. "Stop it! That's not what those are for!"

"Then why do they call them *throw* pillows?" asks Anthony.

Allison cracks up.

I force myself not to smile. "Okay, okay… fine. You three are staying in town."

They all nod.

Maybe it's evil of me, but I don't say anything about winter coats or warm clothes. I want them 'stuck' in the pizza place, unable to go outside and do something stupid. We grab hands and I fixate on the screen showing the small blue building. The ground's covered in snow. Can't even tell where the roads are—or if this place *has* roads. It might all be dirt under the snow. Honestly, this 'town' looks like a bunch of huge shacks clustered together in the frozen tundra.

"Wait," says Tammy. "Let me start blocking before you go. I'm gonna be in like a trance while doing this, so I won't be able to do anything else… or really be aware of what's going on around me."

Anthony picks her up. "I got ya."

My daughter closes her eyes. A moment later, a strange sensation slides over my brain. Allison thinks we're wearing 'brain condoms' now. I'm about to poke her for thinking the word around my kids, but Tammy smiles. I get the sense she'd have laughed but she's too focused. Dammit. My kid finds condom jokes funny. The world is already over.

Don't be so melodramatic. Okay, you guys are as protected as I can get. Mom, this is going to mess with your powers a little.

How so?

I've built a telepathic wall around our heads. It's like we're stealth bombers. Elizabeth —or any telepath—won't be able to 'see' us unless they're almost on top of us. But, using your mind powers is gonna feel like running in mud.

All right. Hopefully, it won't be too much of an issue.

I focus on the screen, picturing the ground behind the little pizza place in Barrow. It's a small, blue building with a chintzy porch more like pallets placed on the ground than an actual porch. The dancing flame appears in my mind, gradually expanding with the same scene inside it... only the snow's a little deeper in my vision. Two guys in thick coats walk by... I wait for them to go inside the pizza place, then mentally pull the flame past us.

It's as though we stand still and the doorway goes by. Reality is every bit as desolate as the picture made it out to be. Snow covers everything. No paved roads. It almost looks like they decided to simply pack all the snow down and drive on top of it. Might explain why most of the cars in sight are Jeeps, 4x4s or trucks, though there is a little Nissan parked by the pizza place. Someone's brave. Even though by time zone we're an hour earlier than home, it's dark out.

Allison yelps from the sudden change in temperature. Anthony drops an F-bomb. Tammy doesn't appear to notice we've gone from our pleasantly warm living room to negative twenty or so degrees in an instant. Thanks to Max's amulet, I don't feel much different. Other than I'm now standing in a stiff breeze, it doesn't feel noticeably colder for me.

"Hurry inside and sit tight," I say.

Anthony jogs to the door of the pizza place, which really looks more like someone's private home—if people lived in windowless wooden shacks. It doesn't open, appearing locked. Oh, we're probably at the back end of the building. Allison rapidly waves her arms around in mystical hand motions while making a face like she just tried to sit on a toilet with the seat up. A brief flicker of amber light surrounds her and the urgency fades from her face. She exhales in relief. Via our mental link, she explains she cast a spell on herself to do the same thing as the amulet Max gave me.

Nice. Can you enchant the kids, too?

"Yeah," says Allison in response to my thought. "And not cool, Sam. Not cool at all."

"No, it isn't cool. It's freezing."

She sticks her tongue out at me. "I meant not

warning us and wanting us to be trapped here. We don't need to be trapped here. Millicent already scared the crap out of me."

"Sorry... just want you guys to be safe—and we're from California. We don't actually own coats heavy enough for this climate anyway."

Allison throws a 'warming' spell on Anthony and Tammy. Still, the three of them hurry into the pizza place out of the wind. If anyone sees me standing around out here in a T-shirt, jeans, and sneakers, they're going to assume me drunk or crazy.

I stretch my wings and leap into the air, climbing up to about a thousand feet or so before looking down. Wow. This town is basically about as far north as it's possible to get without leaving Alaska for the ocean. Seems to be split in two major sections around a giant lake, with a single, large runway going east-to-west at the southernmost edge of town. Doesn't look like any residences exist south of the runway, just a handful of industrial properties.

It's doubtful Elizabeth put her operation anywhere close to town, though even she isn't likely to tolerate extremes of temperature for long. The land to the south is riddled with huge frozen lakes and only a few signs of humanity. I doubt anyone in Barrow will remember seeing mysterious black vans or anything unusual given the way the protection spell has been making people forget and erasing Post-It notes. With Tammy presently suppressing my mind powers (for good reason), I'm going to have to do this the hard way and fly out to check each building or property in person.

"Well, Elizabeth wanted remote. This qualifies." I set my fists against my hips and narrow my eyes. "Okay, bitch. Where are you…?"

Chapter Twenty-One
The Hotel Ascendant

I fly back and forth, visiting a couple of quarries and commercial properties, though it's difficult to tell from the air what sort of businesses they are. Going on the assumption Elizabeth isn't going to attempt hiding near ordinary people doing ordinary things, I keep searching.

A few miles south from Barrow, I spot a facility that appears to be an abandoned military base attached to a small runway of its own. Tire marks in the snow suggest an aircraft has landed there somewhat recently, though the plane must be in one of the hangar-style buildings out of sight. Another thing I find odd are the six or seven people walking around in ordinary clothing—mostly turtlenecks and black pants. Definitely not appropriate attire for negative twenty degrees.

Bingo. This must be the place.

I turn toward the facility and glide the last half mile or so as quietly as possible. My ears are significantly more sensitive than a mortal's, a trait it's wise to assume Elizabeth's people also share. These angel wings aren't as loud as Talos's wings, but they still do make *some* noise. Fortunately, there's a bit of wind out here tonight. It's howling enough to mask the flutter of feathers.

When I'm about 300 yards away from the base, the people moving around outside start to appear as if outlined in energy. Each one of them has a shimmering, white aura peeling up from their bodies like fire. It's more obvious to me in person than on the security video, and somewhat reminds me of the way ghosts appear when they want me to see them—only the figure inside the glowing part is quite solid.

It's about this time I really start not liking the idea these 'ascendant dark masters' as Max called them have so much power it's literally leaking out of their bodies. I fly over a razor-wire fence surrounding the place and come in for a landing behind the smaller of the two hangar buildings, using it to block myself from the rest of the compound.

The condition of the building makes me think the Army (or maybe Air Force) abandoned the base back in the sixties. It may still be an active federal property, and thus off limits, but Elizabeth is definitely not one to care much about mortal laws.

I hurry to my right, approaching a small door along the rear wall. It's locked, and I don't feel like making the kind of noise busting the door would generate. Wind howl can cover only so much. Cracking metal is going to be obvious to half a dozen dark masters. I keep going to the corner and peek around at more snow-covered ground. The large hangar's main doors are closed, and windowless. However, a smaller door to the right of them reveals lights on inside. The only building here that doesn't look like a hangar—a one-story rectangle—has windows, but no lights on. I'm guessing it held the barracks, mess hall, and basically everything else for this extremely remote outpost. No idea why Elizabeth didn't use it, but it looks empty.

Might be a trick, though.

I move to another building, and find myself creeping along the side of the small hangar to a little square window. It's too grimy for me to see inside, so I concentrate on mentally projecting myself forward out of my body, sticking my metaphorical head through the wall. The hanger contains a single Leer jet. Doesn't appear to be anything else in there. I'm about to dismiss this building as useless when the crunch of someone walking toward the front corner outside spooks me. I teleport into the hangar, next to the plane. The person about to walk around the corner couldn't possibly have seen me.

Whew.

A flutter of fabric at my left announces a man running at me. Well, more like leaping. My instincts kick in, boosting my reflexes way beyond human capability in an instant—and the guy is *still* moving frighteningly fast. He crashes into me, knocking me flat on my back before I can even process the reality of being under attack. His body is almost stonelike under his clothes, though he doesn't weigh any more than a normal guy should—an important fact.

The guy goes to tear out my throat with his teeth, clearly mistaking me for a normal mortal.

Admittedly, my reflexes didn't do much for me yet other than allow me to actually see the guy before we collided. A normal person would've been dead not knowing what the hell hit them.

I shove the guy hard enough to launch him straight up almost to the ceiling.

In a second our accelerated reflexes stretch out to feel more like six, he hangs eighteen feet above me, staring down with a mixture of annoyance, confusion, and finally realization. He kinda looks like one of the terrorists from *Die Hard,* vaguely Eastern European, arrogant, and not in a great mood. I'm not sure if he recognizes *me* personally or merely figured out I'm not a normal person. The shimmery white glow clinging to him intensifies as his emotions shift toward anger.

I'm obviously not an ascendant dark master, so I must be destroyed.

At least, according to him.

His grin shifts malevolent and he extends his fingernails out to four-inch claws. Blond hair flutters around his head as he falls back toward me. I probably should get the hell out of the way, but I do something risky and potentially stupid: stay put.

He's so focused on my face/neck, he doesn't pay any attention to what I'm doing with my hands. I get my sword out of its pocket dimension and hold it straight up above my chest. The guy rears his hand back to rip at my neck on his way down. For a hundredth of a second that feels like two, he seems to notice the blade in my hands—but he's got nowhere to go. Gravity's a bitch, and he ain't got wings as the song says.

No, I'm kidding. Not a song. Just made that up.

The ascendant lands on the Devil Killer, impaling himself all the way to the cross-guard with a sensation like I'm stabbing dense glue. Flames belch out of the wound, his skin igniting on contact with the angelic steel. His knees hit me in the legs, his arms erupt in a spasmodic flailing. I throw him to the side before he thinks to shred my arms. He hits the concrete floor on his back and slides a few yards, still convulsing and twitching. Black sludge wells up out of his mouth as well as the fairly small wound in his chest.

The Devil Killer got him right in the heart.

I raise the sword to finish him off with a beheading stroke—hey the guy did attack me first without so much as a warning—but he explodes into a cloud of dusty ash and spectral energy. The whorl of glowing light rising from the dusty smear of remains twists into a sideways tornado funnel, and keeps compressing further, becoming a narrow strand connected to the tip of my blade.

It's as though the Devil Killer *eats* him.

Too stunned to do anything else, I stand there holding the weapon in both hands, staring dumbstruck as the blade heats up to an orange forge-glow. After a few seconds, the light show ends. Only a pile of flaming clothing remains of the guy.

I stare at my sword. The heat radiating from it is almost powerful enough to make me want to put it down. Okay, that's different. Never did this before… but I've also never killed a dark master before either. Part of me wants to say this guy was on the weaker end of the spectrum. Or at least the foolish end. He mistook me for a mortal and tried to feed on me. I'm going to assume Tammy's shielding my mind is how he failed to realize what/who I am.

Can't count on them all making the same mistake.

Waving the sword around cools the blade enough for it to stop glowing. The sword's reaction, more than anything, tells me these ascendant masters have a lot of power bottled up inside them. Or maybe this effect is normal for ending a dark master. Usually, they slink back to the Void if a vampire, werewolf, or whatever is destroyed, but this really feels like ol' Hans here got a one-way ticket back to the Origin.

Is it a side effect of whatever Elizabeth did to bring them out of the Void and generate bodies for themselves or am I wielding one of the few ways to really kill dark masters? I've known that some of the escaped dark masters can take on temporary physical forms. Closer to ectoplasmic ghosts than anything. Dark masters are truly without bodies, which is why they need to possess. These ascendant blokes seem to have a permanent body. Which, I suspect, is what makes them ascendant—and why the fireworks display when killed.

The more important thing here is I managed to neutralize this guy before we made a bunch of noise. How do I know no one noticed this? Simple: there aren't a dozen more ascendant dark masters kicking down the doors.

I've learned a few things during our brief fight. These guys are dangerously fast. It makes sense why Millicent warned me about Allison and Tammy. Neither are any faster, stronger, or tougher than ordinary humans. They'd be dead before even realizing something attacked them. The Fire Warrior is also no faster than an ordinary human, but he's tough... and so much bigger than them. And, you know, fire.

Right, standing here gawking at my weapon like a thirteen-year-old boy finding a 'real sword' at a renaissance festival isn't going to help anyone. I put the Devil Killer back in the dimension pocket and slip out the back door of the hangar.

At the corner, I peek around enough to see the big hangar across the runway. Lots of open space, but a quick teleport covers 400 yards in an instant. I appear in front of the small door and hurry inside, hoping none of the ascendant ones patrolling the tarmac saw me. As far as I know, teleportation is a fairly rare ability among vampires. I've got to begrudgingly thank Elizabeth for it. Different dark masters bring slightly different abilities to the vampires they make. Or maybe it's Jeffcock I should be thanking? Hmm. I like that better, even if untrue.

Or, hell. For all I know, things vampires can do are completely random. Still, Elizabeth is a ridiculously powerful telepath. Her gift in that regard made my mental powers stronger than the average vampire. I mean, this bitch is so strong merely being around her for fourteen years is what's made Tammy into the telepathic enigma she is. Kinda like how if you leave a piece of metal near a titanic electromagnet long enough, it becomes a permanent magnet.

Anyway, the room inside the door of the big hangar is fairly ordinary looking. I'm in a small office with three steel desks from the 1960s. Old posters on the walls warn of 'Russian ears being everywhere.' Looks like this used to be an Air Force base, or outpost. Maybe a testing ground. I read somewhere they used remote places like this for experimental nuclear power reactors back in those days. Send a crew of like eight guys to the middle of nowhere and see how long they can keep a tiny reactor going.

Considering there are no power cables connecting this place back to Barrow, the lights in the hallway past this office are either magical or there is a nuclear reactor nearby. I kinda hope it's magic. A mini-reactor from sixty years ago is probably not the safest thing in the world.

I creep over to the door, flatten myself against the wall, and peek through the window.

The scene in front of me is *not* what I expected by any stretch of the imagination.

Red carpet, dark wood furniture, statues, bookshelves… and iron bars.

It's basically a movie set taking up roughly one-sixth of the space inside the hangar, reminiscent of 1940s England, like someone tried to recreate Winston Churchill's office, or something close to it. Five separate square 'rooms' are arranged in a grid, each one surrounded by prison-style bars. Though they appear functionally 'cells,' it's hard to think of them that way due to their size. Each one is as big as a spacious old-timey office, including a small private bathroom in one corner, a bed, huge desk, bookshelves, globes, fancy divans, a wet bar… wow. If not for each space being surrounded by metal bars, this would be a five-star hotel.

Old-fashioned oil burning lamps appear to be the only sources of light inside. Maybe I'm wrong on both counts: neither magic nor nuclear-provided electricity. However, there appear to be computers on each desk, an anachronistic clash with the rest of the scenery. Okay, so electricity *is* here. Don't have time to waste on figuring out where it's coming from. I need to get the people out as fast as possible.

I spot Zandra Adams seated at one of the desks, typing furiously at the computer. Quentin Adams is in another 'room,' also working at his computer. To be honest, I'd never have recognized him unless I'd researched this case.

And oh yeah. I need to return his high school story.

The third prison-office holds a thirtysomething Indian woman. She's got a larger computer screen in front of her, and appears to be drawing or writing directly on it with a pen. Probably a stylus. I'm guessing she's some manner of illustrator. The chamber behind Quentin's contains several electronic pianos and a set of drum pads. A scrawny man with a pointy chin, long, black hair, and a frustrated scowl sits at the desk. Wow, I didn't think musicians still tried to pull off the 'rock star' look.

In the fifth room, an older man sits at the desk with his feet up, hands folded in his lap. I can't tell if he's thinking or protesting. Tammy's mental shield is getting in the way of me reading his mind from here, but it's not too important. Though, this guy looks kinda familiar. I stare at him for a few seconds until it clicks—it's Lance Blackburn.

Okay, my daughter fangirled over Quentin. Now it's my turn. This guy's one of the top three Hollywood movie directors. He's the guy who directed *Simulacrum*, the space movie where the crippled former soldier virtually inhabits a fake alien body to spy on a primitive society... and ends up leading them to revolution against the humans who've gone there to exploit the planet.

Little preachy, but I love his movies.

Don't recognize the musician or the Indian woman. Then again, I wouldn't recognize a musician more recent than twenty years ago, and illustrators aren't usually famous. It's almost too good to be true not to see even one ascendant dark master in this hangar. All the space between the 'offices' is open, carpeted like the hallway in a 1940s British hotel, only flanked by prison bars instead of walls. There's at least two stories of open air above the top of the cells. Behind the 'movie set' is mostly empty space except for the crumbling remains of an old military transport plane. The thing doesn't look like it's moved in decades, nor will it go anywhere under its own power again.

Okay, this should be a lot easier than I thought. Walk in, grab creator, teleport. Rinse, repeat. Wait, no. I'll wear myself out fast. Better I bend bars and teleport them all at once.

I ease the door open and step into the hangar-slash-movie set.

Zandra and Quentin look up as I walk down the 'corridor' between their cells. The woman drawing on her monitor is too into her work to notice me, as is Mr. Rock Star. Lance, two cells away on the right side, lifts his head to stare at me. He seems both confused and intrigued, as if he knows I shouldn't be here but doesn't have a clue what to make of me.

I approach the bars on the left, by Zandra's 'office.' Never in my life have I seen a jail cell bigger than my living room. It's even got a 'roof' of bars. Elizabeth must have used magic to create all of this. I couldn't imagine the cost of shipping all this nice old furniture out here to the middle of freakin' nowhere the normal way.

"Shh," I whisper, grasping the bars. "I'm here to help."

"Are you now?" asks Elizabeth.

I look to my right as she walks out into view past the far corner of Zandra's cell, strolling down the carpeted faux corridor as casually as can be. She's rolling with the Forties theme, rocking an off-the-shoulder sparkling lavender gown like something belonging in a vintage private eye film.

"Damn." I bonk my head on the bars. "Too good to be true is *always* too good to be true."

Chapter Twenty-Two
Better This Way

Elizabeth sashays up to me, stopping a step out of arm's reach.

Like the others, she, too, has a faint shimmering aura around her body. The sequins in her gown appear to catch the light, making her look like a galaxy took human form. She's definitely proof that a gorgeous outside doesn't mean the inside's pretty, too. Her casually moving so close to me is either overconfidence or a big red flag. Hoping it's the former, but I'm worried enough not to pounce on her.

"Let me guess," I say. "I don't have a chance of stopping you? Or are you about to tell me I'm too late?"

She emits a haughty laugh, trying to make me feel like a simpleton who just did something cute. "I was going to tell you it's too late to stop us from creating our own universe. Oh, Samantha. Always trying to steal my fun."

"Kidnapping people isn't fun," I grumble, staring at my hands gripping the bars. Should I still bend them so Zandra can get out? Seems kinda pointless now.

"No." Elizabeth waves dismissively. "I'm talking about our little conversation here. Becoming empress of an entire reality made just for me isn't just 'fun,' it's practical."

"An entire reality? I'll admit, I thought you were just going for a world. Go big, or go home, eh?"

She purses her lips. "Somehow, you've defied the memory charm."

"Don't be too impressed, I haven't a clue how I did it."

She chuckles. "Your connection to me is likely the reason my spell didn't affect you. Our essences share certain similarities that inadvertently fooled the magic into thinking you and I are the same. Well, for the most part. I see you nearly forgot that you could teleport great distances based on a photo. Too bad."

"Is this you trying to bait me into saying

something lame like 'we'll never be the same?'" I ask.

"Classic line," says Zandra.

"Schlock," mutters Lance, too low for Zandra to hear, though Elizabeth smiles.

"I thought they stopped using that line in Eighties action movies?" says the musician.

"They did, Tyson," says Lance at a normal volume.

Elizabeth makes this beleaguered 'see what I have to put up with' face. I half expect her to call them bickering children.

I let go of the bars, face her, and hold up one finger. "Okay, hold on a moment here. So our guess is right? You're seriously forcing a bunch of creators to make an entirely new dimension for you to inhabit and take all of your dark master loyalists with you out of this one?"

She raises one eyebrow. "Yes. And you are too late to stop me."

"Little flat," calls Lance. "Try it again with more energy. You're supposed to be the powerful evil mastermind talking down to the Jane Bond character."

Elizabeth clenches her jaw.

I want to laugh. Somehow, I manage not to, probably because my laughter might kill Lance. Gotta hand it to him. Even in the midst of a ridiculous and dangerous situation, he's still acting like the A-list Hollywood director he is.

I strike a pose and try my best naïve, innocent hero voice. "Your plan can never work, Elizabeth. It's doomed to failure from the start, and I won't let you harm these people."

"Nice," says Zandra.

The Indian girl rolls her eyes at me.

Lance scratches at his eyebrow. "Is this going spoof comedy now?"

"Yeah." I give him a thumbs-up before looking back to Elizabeth. "Seriously, though. Your goal is to *leave* this world, right?"

Frowning, Elizabeth folds her arms. "Is there a particular reason you keep repeating the same question?"

"Yeah. I'm struggling to believe it. I spent the past thirteen years thinking I was the only thing standing between you and conquering *this* world."

"Is the brunette a vampire, too?" asks the Indian girl, apparently to Lance.

"How should I know?" He shrugs. "I didn't write her in."

"She's not mine," says Zandra.

"Well, don't look at me. I do theme albums." Tyson paces around in his office. "Until you guys agree on the overall aesthetic of this setting, I can't even start on the background music."

Elizabeth makes a 'wait a sec' gesture at me, then spins to look at him. "You're not here to make background music. This is not a movie project. As stated before, you are to flesh out the various musical influences for each of the cultures inhabiting the world."

"And I can't do that until these guys give me some fictional cultures to work with." Tyson holds his hands out to either side. "Zandra and Lance are at two totally opposite ends and Quentin keeps adding political intrigue and warring kingdoms. The only reason Ramani is making concept art is she doesn't care what the writers are doing."

"Trying to give you three some ideas," says the Indian girl.

"Wow." I set my hands on my hips and exhale. "I'm impressed. Okay. So, Elizabeth…"

She twists, fixing me with this glare like she's about to try giving me a facelift with no prior surgical training or tools.

I say, "If your plan is really to leave to another world-slash-dimension and take all of your dark master friends with you, I can't honestly justify getting in your way. It's more or less what I want: you not taking over *this* world and no longer being a threat to those I love. As long as you don't intend to hurt these creators, fine. Whatever. Knock yourself out."

The hostility in her face lessens. "I find it difficult to believe you aren't going to attempt to interfere."

"You spent long enough inside my head to know how I think. As far as 'Elizabeth' is concerned, the only thing I've ever wanted to do was stop you from destroying or conquering *this* world. You're the one who made me believe I had to contain you in order to do that. If you're really going to make an entirely new world and go there, I'm fine with it."

"You're going to let her kidnap us?" barks Quentin.

I look at him. "Only temporarily. If the five of you are able to create an entire world out of thin air and she goes there and disappears forever—and you five are alive afterward? Yes. The lesser of two evils. I have no idea what her plans are, but I won't let her kill any of you."

The creators look at each other. They don't like it. Then again, there may be no other choice either.

"Just don't think of it as being kidnapped," I say. "More like being temporarily drafted for the greater good. Trust me, it's better this way."

"Hmm." Elizabeth narrows her eyes at me. "Of course you'll understand if I don't fully trust you. I did not foresee you helping me."

"Hang on." I raise a hand. "*Not* getting in your way and 'helping' you aren't exactly the same things. I'm only here to make sure these people all get to go home alive."

Elizabeth walks off down the fake corridor between cells. "I'm afraid you'll have a rather boring wait, in that case, but you're free to watch. Care for tea?"

Unable to believe myself for agreeing to see where this goes, I follow her to the last part of the 'movie set,' where they've set up tables and chairs in the general style of a late-Forties lounge. A fair distance away out in the middle of the bare concrete hangar floor, a giant stone ring tall enough to drive a pickup truck through stands atop a glowing runic power circle. I assume it's going to become the gateway through which Elizabeth and her minions leave the world behind.

Elizabeth takes a seat at a round table. "You may as well sit, Samantha. This is going to take a little time."

Never in my life did I imagine sitting cordially at a table with this woman. It's still a bit of a shock she's outside of my head and in her own physical body. That aside, my expectations for our meeting had been way more apocalyptic than drinking tea while listening to a bunch of creative people argue behind us.

My life is weird.

Chapter Twenty-Three
The Sixth Creator

So... I'm sitting at a table with the woman I've spent years regarding as the most evil creature in the world. Perhaps second to whoever invented the annoying USB plug. But still. Here I am having tea with Elizabeth while five people she kidnapped are locked inside prison cells... and I'm not tearing bars down. Yet.

What's a little kidnapping for the sake of saving the world?

"You've changed more than I expected, Samantha." She smiles before sipping from her teacup. "I am having to expend considerable effort to see your thoughts."

"Didn't think it would be a good idea to let

you see me coming from miles away."

"You planned to do what? 'Rescue' these people out from under my nose? To what end?" She laughs. "I merely would have collected them again. Or others. There are many such creators, though these five have skill sets that I desire."

"Hey, you know me. Had to try."

"No need thinking about silly dancing frogs, dear. I already know my son is planning to bring his insufferable friends here. He will be too late."

I shrug. "Again, if you're really going to just leave this world behind, I don't see why he'd try to stop you either."

"Unlike you, my dear, Maximillian would want to 'save' the occupants of my new world, too. You, at least, have the intelligence to realize they would not exist without me."

I start to drink tea when it hits me *she* is sipping tea, as well. Okay, so the ascendant masters aren't pure bloodsuckers anymore either. "I had the same argument with myself, but is it really any different from a writer putting their characters through hardships?"

"Characters do not exist. My world will."

A thought occurs to me. "Where's Dracula? And Cornelius? Are they still one and the same?"

"Ah, those two. Yes, they still share a body. Apparently, Dracula has proven rather difficult to dispose of. No matter, Cornelius has designs of his own... on this world."

"What sort of designs?"

"You'll have to ask him. But this much I know, he doesn't want to follow me off world. Which is just as well. There can be only one supreme being, right?"

"If you say so." Then again, I suspect the man realized just how terrible a world might be ruled by Elizabeth. "So how long does it take to create a world?"

"I can do it in a few days," yells Zandra, "but Quentin here takes three years to write *one* book. He's been stuck in Estaeron for so damn long, he's having trouble thinking of any new ideas."

Tyson chuckles.

"My dear Zandra," says Quentin in a bored tone, "screenwriters do not understand anything about crafting novels *or* the worlds behind them."

Lance lowers his feet off his desk, stands, and begins to pace around. "We screenwriters leave all the tedious parts to the set designers. Only a fool spends four pages describing the damn pottery in the background."

"Only two paragraphs!" shouts Quentin. "The Zhaveesi people place great cultural importance on the patterns they craft into their pottery. The subtle curves, notches, and dots within each line they etch into the clay represents significant moments in—"

"This is why it takes him three years per book," says Zandra.

"I like the depth." Ramani stretches, yawning. "But I don't like having to wait so long for the story to continue."

The creators proceed to throw ideas back and forth about the world they're working on for Elizabeth. How many continents, how many individual civilizations, names of nations and so on. Ramani decides to tell the others she's going to start doing concept art for flowers and plants unique to each region. Tyson asks the others to omit insects entirely because 'they are annoying.' Quentin flat out refuses, saying they're a vital part of the ecosystem. Then they all start arguing if scientific accuracy is important.

"Have they been arguing like this the entire time?"

Elizabeth's eyelids half close. "You have no idea."

I look around at the hangar, the portal-to-be, the dead cargo plane, the fake 1940s 'hotel,' tapping my foot on air. Yeah, this is surreal. It's like James Bond and Dr. No having a cordial brunch after finding unlikely common ground.

"So how has life been treating you since I moved out?" asks Elizabeth.

"Can't complain too much. Finally managed to take a vacation."

"Oh? Do tell?" She raises her eyebrows. "Fun?"

"That's one word for it. We went to Europe."

She blinks. "How did you afford that? Last I checked, we didn't exactly live the life of luxury."

"I'm not as poor as I used to be."

"Finally trying to become the vampire you should have been all along?" Elizabeth smiles.

"Not really. Unexpected inheritance. I still haven't figured out how most old vampires are so rich."

"You are such an ingénue, Samantha." She clucks her tongue at me. "Even if, by Hollywood standards, you're now an old maid, you've still got the naiveté. Vampires are wealthy because we take what we desire, and use all the powers we have to achieve our goals.

You think Nelson Rockefeller was mortal?"

"I did… But, wait a sec. Didn't he die?"

"The identity did. Not the man behind it. Spend a lifetime or two looting corporations or exploiting workers and you'll have more money than you know what to do with."

"You and your fucking goblins," shouts Lance behind us.

"What's wrong with goblins?" barks Quentin. "You'd rather add some giant blue alien tribals?"

I cringe.

"Children, please!" yells Zandra. "The sooner we create a cohesive world, the sooner we return to our normal lives."

Elizabeth, whether she means to or not, does a spot-on impression of the Kermit the Frog sipping tea meme. It's as though she's amused, but this *is* her circus and these *are* her monkeys. I almost get the feeling it amuses her to have them bickering so much. Maybe she thinks the discord will make for a darker universe, just the way she likes it.

"Wouldn't you have better luck *hiring* them rather than abducting them?" I ask her.

"Initially, we mind-controlled them. Things were going smoothly, but it turns out the part of them responsible for their being actual creators doesn't work when under mental domination. Stifles creativity."

I chuckle. "Yeah. Even I knew that. Mind controlling people turns them into automatons, even more so than working a call center job. Have you tried a simple compulsion to 'work together'?"

All five creators stare at me.

"Hmm." Elizabeth taps a finger to her chin. "You might be on to something."

I look at them, holding my arms out to either side. "What? I'm trying to get you out of here and home as fast as possible."

They exchange glances.

"You're telling her to mind-control us," yells Ramani. "Not cool."

Elizabeth tilts her head. "Perhaps I misjudged you. Never imagined *you* capable of forcing people to work against their will for your interest."

"It's not my interest. It's in theirs—going home." I bite back the urge to compare them to unruly toddlers. Quentin's about my age while Zandra and Lance are older than me. Also, referring to them as children is something Elizabeth would do.

"Don't let their minor disagreements worry you." Elizabeth leans back in her chair. "Creation is filled with opposing forces. If all energy flowed in the same direction, their world would not be alive. Besides, the world they are crafting is much farther along than it sounds, or they suspect."

"How is it even possible for them to be ahead of where they think they are?"

"I have other things in motion." She bats her eyelashes at me. "Tell me about your vacation?"

I'm probably going to regret it, but we can't just sit here staring at each other. Like I'm making small-talk with a coworker I'm not particularly fond of, I start rambling about our trip. We both end up laughing at the sheer insanity of something going supernaturally wrong almost everywhere I went. It's beyond surreal to see this woman I've feared and loathed for so long laughing at my stories about Tammy and Anthony.

The strangest thing ever to happen in my life so far is me starting to see Elizabeth as an actual person and not some blacker-than-black source of all evil.

"Like, for real? I'm not the only supernatural being on the planet. Why did it feel like those places saved up their weird until I got there to set it loose?"

Elizabeth starts to sip tea, but realizes her

cup is empty. "Because there are forces at work in the background, too esoteric for even me to directly control. But I have learned how to read them. The demon attack is understandable given what you've done with their plans, but the rest of it could have been avoided simply by minding your own business."

"You're saying these things happened because 'forces beyond my understanding' knew I couldn't simply walk away?"

"Something like that, yes." She stops smiling and looks at me. "You want to ask me something."

"I, um..."

"Go ahead. We're presently under a white flag."

She knows I've been thinking about her reaction to stories about my kids. Far more ordinary than I'd ever expected her to be. Then again, if certain rumors are to be believed, this woman once murdered girls younger than Tammy to bathe in their blood.

The face she makes at me thinking it doesn't say truth or fiction. I suppose she enjoys the mystery.

"I'm kind of astonished you're finding cute kid stories funny. How did you handle Max leading an army against you?"

"I'll answer your question with a question. He's still alive, isn't he?" She glances off to the side.

Oh, wow. Now *there* is a side of Elizabeth I never expected to see. If her body language means anything, she couldn't bring herself to kill her son. Dammit. She keeps this up, I'm going to start thinking of her as a person. Of course, she could be playing me. She did, after all, convince me I was the savior of the world and walked me right into a confrontation with the Red Rider.

No, I don't regret killing him. The bastard deserved it.

A loud, electric buzz comes from the stone ring by the portal. Runes carved into its surface glow brilliant purplish-white. Three lightning arcs leap from the inner surface of the circle, striking the ground a few feet away. Another crackling spark jumps straight up, coalescing into a strange creature made of light and plasma. It's about seven feet tall with a head that looks like a combination between a jellyfish and a flying saucer. Multiple swaths of silky 'fabric' hang down like curtains, sorta forming the impression of a body wearing a robe, only the garment is empty. It has no true eyes, arms, or legs, but something about the geometry of its crystalline face gives a sense it's gazing in a particular direction.

The instant it appears, my skin prickles like I'm standing too close to a broken microwave with faulty shielding.

I jump to my feet. "What the f—?"

"Calm yourself, Samantha. This is Azoth."

Silent except for the continuous crackle of energy, the being glides across the hangar to us.

"Their language is based on electromagnetic modulation," says Elizabeth. "Only two percent of it is even audible to our ears. Azoth is the name I use."

"Oh. What is he… or she?"

"Azoth is Azoth. A being from the ninth dimension. They don't have genders, dear. Nor do they care if we refer to them with or without one." She grins like Dr. Evil about to reveal the best part of the sinister plan. "Behold, the sixth creator. He will be doing most of the work."

I lean back, staring way up at the hangar roof—and a whole bunch of dead gas lamps. "Ahh. Now I understand how your world is further along than it seemed. A ninth dimensional creator? Several times exponentially more powerful."

Elizabeth nods once. "He will be able to create a fully realized third-dimensional world in roughly four minutes."

"Wow. So, you and all the dark masters with you are going to be away from Earth in less than an hour?"

"That is correct." Elizabeth stands.

"Can I ask a stupid question?"

"If it is stupid, why would you seek to find an answer?" asks Azoth in a somewhat robotic voice neither completely male nor truly female. It strikes me somewhat closer to male, so maybe I'll think of this being as a he for simplicity's sake. Especially if their people don't care.

"Curiosity," I say, then look at Elizabeth. "How did you convince a ninth-dimensional being to help you?"

Elizabeth frowns off to the side. "He will be a supreme god in our new world."

I raise both eyebrows, stunned. "Someone higher than you?"

She sighs dismissively. "Sacrifices must be made. For now."

"Are the others prepared?" asks Azoth.

"Yes. They have gathered enough ideas to suit their purposes." Elizabeth gestures toward the large cells, where the five human creators all stand gob-smacked at the sight of this being from six dimensions above ours.

Something tells me Lance Blackburn's next movie is going to feature aliens with a strong resemblance to Azoth—assuming, of course, we all get out of here intact.

The dimensional being glides past me, entering the hallway. He stops at the four-way corridor intersection between Quentin, Zandra, Ramani, and Tyson's cells. Lance's 'office' is behind Tysons, closer to Elizabeth and me.

"Tell him everything you have created thus far," calls Elizabeth in a commanding voice. "Show him your artwork. Allow him to hear your music. It will not confuse him if you all talk at once."

Oh, this I have to see...

Tyson hits a button on his computer, filling the air with epic music perfect for the background score of a grim medieval fantasy movie. Honestly, it sounds like he's borrowed from the *Contest of Sovereignty* miniseries. Doubtful Elizabeth cares about copyright infringement. I don't think he's lifted the exact song, but the mood's the same.

While the music blares, Ramani pivots her monitor toward Azoth and begins showing him digital paintings of various people, spanning multiple ethnicities and costumes. Quentin, Zandra, and Lance all read from their notes. It's maddening trying to follow Quentin talking about the inner workings of various noble houses and strata of society while Zandra's describing creatures and beasts with the enthusiasm of a child. Lance appears to be giving a rundown of different countries and their political relationships with each other as well as the everpresent conflict between the greedy advanced societies and the poor but determined natives.

Azoth floats there, seemingly unfazed by the heavy bombardment of imagery and words.

Even Elizabeth is kinda cringing at the barrage of info.

Ramani's monitor switches from humans to plants and animals—but nothing that could eat people. Monsters are Zandra's area of expertise, apparently. She's loading this place up with fantasy creatures like wyverns and manticores. Eek. Quentin shifts gears from noble house politics to talking about the magic of the world. I assumed Elizabeth would want a reality where magic had more than average power. The type of place where people do the Allison thing and throw bolts of power from their hands all the time.

As the minutes tick by, thin strands of energy reach out from Azoth like the tentacles of a jellyfish, encircling the creators one by one. It's almost like he's plugging in a wire to download the contents of their brains. The people don't appear to notice it, almost as if they've been pulled into a trancelike state, compelling them to talk ceaselessly about their work. Amazingly, they're not trying to shout over each other, resulting in a completely indecipherable mess.

I'm about to stick my fingers in my ears.

Azoth emits a brilliant flash, his 'body' oscillating between multiple different poses in snap-flashes like a weird video trick from a low budget ghost movie.

Tyson's head explodes into a fine red mist.

His body thuds to the floor.

A second later, I shout, "Holy F—" but I'm drowned out by the roar of an explosion coming from Azoth. The energy shockwave knocks me back into the table I'd been sitting at, over it, and to the floor. Elizabeth hits the ground as well, sliding beside me toward the rune circle.

I lay there for a moment, staring up at a haze of smoke between me and the ceiling. It occurs to me the hangar has become completely silent. I can't even hear myself breathing. Actually, the hangar isn't silent—I've gone deaf.

Elizabeth taps me on the arm. She's still lying flat on her back beside me, though she's turned her head toward me. Her lips move. I'm not the best lip-reader in the world, but it appears she's asking me if I can hear anything.

I shake my head.

She scowls, frustrated… and more than a little worried.

I take it the creator from a higher dimension was not supposed to explode.

Shit! The people!

Other than my eardrums being blown out, I don't feel hurt. Sitting up isn't too difficult. The movie set area is more or less intact, though most of the cell bars have warped like they'd been made out of chocolate and left in the sun a little too long. Some of the wooden furniture has also shifted, twisting and stretching into set pieces from a trippy Alice in Wonderland type story.

Scraps of burning paper float everywhere like ashy snow.

Sadly, Tyson Rimmer is beyond saving.

Zandra, Quentin, Ramani, and Lance all seem to be alive, slightly scorched, and holding their ears.

Azoth has become a lump of glowing lavender jelly about the size of what a wheelbarrow would hold. Steam rises from the muck. Is he dead or unconscious? I can't get any sense of an intelligent mind inside the goo, but Tammy is still shielding me. I didn't sense his thoughts *before* he blew up.

Amid a rushing noise like I'm surfacing out of water, my ability to hear returns. Cool. My eardrums have regrown. Tyson's music is still playing. A continuous electrical crackling comes from the jelly blob.

"Samantha?" asks Elizabeth. "Are you still deaf?"

"Nope. I'm guessing your alien wasn't supposed to pop."

"Most certainly not." She dusts herself off.

The woman's giving off a scary amount of bad energy right now. She's clearly furious, but it's the kind of fury with no responsible party to direct it upon. This is the sort of rage that caused random servants in Caesar's court to be sentenced to death because they happened to be standing too close to the emperor when he needed to vent.

"What happened?" shouts Elizabeth.

"Do you think they overloaded him?" I ask.

Lance wheezes, pushing himself up to sit. He swipes a scrap of smoking paper off his face. "It isn't going to work. We cannot do what you want."

Elizabeth storms over to his cell. "How do

you know that? You're a mere human."

"We touched its mind," says Ramani, not bothering to get up. The way she's kissing the rug behind her desk reminds me of the party where I scraped Tammy and her friends off the floor. "We saw *everything* in a split second. Thousands of worlds flashed before us."

Elizabeth rips the bars on Tyson's office out of her way, grabs his corpse by two fistfuls of his blazer jacket, and shakes him. "Why are you dead? It's not going to work without all of you."

Whoa, okay. She's so angry she's not thinking at all. Does she expect a headless body to answer?

"It won't work *with* all of us." Zandra wearily rises to her feet. "Tyson was a musician driven to create for the beauty of his music as well as his stories. Every one of his projects was a concept album. The songs told a story from the first track to the last. He felt his work passionately. The rest of us, we somewhat distance ourselves from it. He let his music into his soul. *Felt* it in a way we do not."

"He had no defense," rasps Quentin. "When that *thing* tried to link us into a single mind, Tyson metaphorically stood naked before the hail of arrows. His mind could not handle it."

Elizabeth throws Tyson's remains over the

desk. "You aren't telling me why you cannot do what I ask."

"It will not work." Lance swoons into his chair, hand to his forehead. "I don't understand why, only that it won't."

The jelly blob twitches.

Azoth the blob emits a noise like an old-fashioned telephone modem. Probably 'ow my effing head' in his native language. The UFO/jellyfish part solidifies out of the mass of glowing lavender goop, but doesn't rise into the air on robes as before. It rotates toward Elizabeth and slurps across the carpet, dragging a mass of gelatinous ooze behind. He's in no way even close to human, but I kinda see him as a really tall dude in a robe who's dragging himself across the floor after being stabbed.

Elizabeth walks up to him.

"The bridge is too unstable," says Azoth. "This world's energy is chaotic. My resonance is incompatible with these life forms. Any reality resulting from this process would destabilize and destroy itself within three units of time you refer to as months."

Elizabeth stares down at Azoth. This is the face Caligula must have made before throwing an epic temper tantrum. I'm tempted to quietly collect the human creators and teleport out, but doing so would require moving. Moving would attract her attention. While I am somewhat nervous about the idea of how a fight between us would go, my hesitation is about ninety percent out of concern for the remaining mortals around us. Since they are now useless to her plans, she wouldn't have any reason to care if they lived or died. Of course, it also means she has no need to keep them as permanent, immortal prisoners to prop up the existence of her world.

"Fix it!" shouts Elizabeth.

One thing about people who plan situations out to the tiniest detail decades in advance: they don't handle catastrophic failure well. Thinking on her feet isn't Elizabeth's strong suit. She's a planner. Give her fifty years to concoct an elaborate scheme and she's a diabolical maestro. Force her into a situation she didn't expect and ask her to figure out what to do in the heat of a moment—she's going to storm around destroying the scenery and having an epic shit fit.

"It is impossible to fix," says Azoth, a faint flicker within the gel accompanying his voice. "The optimal course of action for you to take is to traverse laterally to an alternate, naturally existing third-dimensional world with conditions similar to this one as it existed roughly two thousand years ago. A primitive realm would allow us to more easily establish ourselves as god and empress."

Elizabeth's rage evaporates to eagerness. "Interesting. How many worlds exist with conditions similar to Earth around Zero BCE?" She walks out of the 'movie set' toward the rune circle.

"6,582," says Azoth.

"Wow," I whisper.

"How many have abundant magic?"

"Twelve." Azoth drags himself after her, gradually rising off the floor into his previously 'floaty' form. "I have located one where society has produced a moderately large empire; however, their technology remains low due to reliance on magic. They have constructed a large city from which you could rule as my agent."

Elizabeth subtly bristles at the suggestion she be a subordinate, even to a ninth-dimensional being. I'm sure she's quietly plotting how to rid herself of having a 'patron,' but for the moment, tolerates it because she's dependent on his assistance. Also, I think I'm right about modern weapons being a bit too powerful for her. Even the most feared army in the Roman Legion—plus wizards—wouldn't survive a tactical nuclear strike. Her only chance to take over the version of Earth I call home would require she conquer so fast no major nation would have the time to mount an effective counterattack. And the odds of setting off a nuclear apocalypse are too high. The earth she may or may not lay claim to might be a wasteland.

She wants to *rule* a world, not turn it into a smoking cinder.

"Very well," says Elizabeth. "Establish a gateway for us. You will be revered as their god and I their empress."

Azoth spins in place, seemingly gazing around. "Sadly, this place is unsuitable to traverse laterally. I will create a doorway to an appropriate location, one powerful enough to connect worlds. Now, summon your allies."

"Umm, Elizabeth?" I jog up behind her. "Are you sure you really want to do that?"

"Quite," she replies, still with her back to me.

"I mean, you seriously want to go take over some innocent other world, enslave its people, and rule as a figurehead empress for a 'god' from the ninth dimension?" I blink.

"Sounds like the plot of one of Zandra's movies," says Lance.

"Mr. Blackburn?" says Zandra, still lying on the floor.

"Yes?" He looks at her.

"Eat a dick."

There's something inherently hilarious about women of a certain age using coarse language. Except I don't have it in me to laugh given we're talking about the conquering of an entire world. It's not much different from what I feared she'd do here to Earth.

"But... it's so primitive there. Won't you miss Starbucks, iPhones, or *Dancing with the Stars*?"

Elizabeth narrows her eyes. "I will admit *Dancing with the Stars* is the kind of cruelty I find appealing. Perhaps I shall inflict it on my new subjects."

"There has to be a way for you to create a new reality. This didn't work, but maybe..."

"There isn't," says Lance, Zandra, Quentin, and Ramani at the same time.

I sigh. "Guys... I'm trying to save a world here."

Azoth approaches the stone ring. Lightning crackles off his body, striking the runes carved around its surface.

"Look, Elizabeth," I say. "You can't just invade and take over an existing civilization."

She glances sideways at me. "You would prefer I do it here? Too much work. A primitive world is far easier to influence."

"No. I'd prefer you didn't do it at all. Why do you have to rule the world, anyway? Maybe just go there and start a coffee shop and grow it until it's on every street corner around the globe. You could control everything without the killing and enslavement part."

"You are amusing, Samantha Moon." Elizabeth almost smiles. "Truth is, I much prefer doing things the old-fashioned way. Those I rule should wail in fear when their empress nears, and consider themselves blessed by the gods if they survive my presence. Besides, the modern world is far too loud and noisy."

"Dammit… wait!" I start to run at Azoth, but Elizabeth is quite a bit faster than I expect.

She spins, catching me across the chest and hurling me off my feet. I fly headfirst for a few seconds before landing on my back hard enough to peel the carpet up from the floor down the aisle between cells. I stop sliding between Quentin and Zandra's 'rooms.'

"Guess it was too good to be true." I sigh.

Elizabeth growls.

"I meant us getting along, me seeing you as an actual person or something." I exhale hard, then sit up.

"Do not think I will tolerate your interference." She points at me. "If you choose to be sentimental and weak about *this* world, it is no longer my concern. As promised, I am leaving it behind. But do not attempt to stop my involvement in the new world. It and everyone in it are mine."

Oh, hell no.

Yeah, I know. Reckless. But I have to at least try to stop her from enslaving an entire lateral dimension.

Chapter Twenty-Four
A Slight Difference of Opinion

Between the warped scenery, the glowing dimensional creature, or facing the event that's haunted my thoughts for years, I'm not sure what makes this moment feel most like a nightmare.

Yeah, it didn't seem likely Elizabeth would stay cordial. It surprised me she even tried to. Not for a second do I think she refrained from attacking me out of any sort of sentimentality, or even laziness. The only reason to make any sense in my mind is she's afraid of me. Not like an 'oh, no, it's Samantha Moon, eek' sort of way... more like I introduce the risk of her plans failing. If she believed she could brush me aside as a triviality, I'm sure a fight would have started a long time ago.

It's curious she didn't finish me off after I barfed her out when I couldn't even stand up on my own, but she might have been as weak as I felt in the moment.

Anyway, her hesitation must prove I have more than a slight chance of winning here. Despite everything, my goal still isn't to destroy her, but to protect the world and everyone in it from her plans. Considering everything I know about her, though, it's probably going to come down to one of us being destroyed. Maybe what she said about her mortal death originally occurring because she couldn't bring herself to harm Max, her son, was a lie. It probably is. She knows I'm too nice for my own good and she's playing me to think of her as a person to make me hesitate even more.

Even if she did truly lack the ability to kill her son, hundreds of years as a dark master would change anyone. I shouldn't allow myself to even pretend she's anything even close to human anymore.

And yet still, I don't want to straight up end her.

I spring to my feet, unsure what to do.

Elizabeth is watching Azoth throw lightning

at the stone ring, no doubt making a portal to the other dimension. It's probably not my job to save *every* world she threatens, but if something like Elizabeth happened to be eyeing this world from afar, I'd sure hope someone in my position at least tried to stop her. Lots and lots of people are going to die and suffer if she succeeds. Her ascendant dark masters would steamroll over any humans in a physical fight.

Attempting to reason with her again isn't going to work. I'd have an easier time trying to talk Kim Kardashian out of buying a new Gucci bag she really wants. Only saving grace there is I doubt she'd torture the purse if it didn't worship her.

Okay, what can I do here?

Hmm, Azoth is mostly electricity…

I pull the Devil Killer out, grab it in a two-handed grip, and swing at one of the bars on Zandra's cell. The nice thing about magical angelic steel is it won't break or even dull when struck against ordinary metal. It also does serious damage. Elizabeth glances at me over her shoulder, but doesn't seem to care. She probably thinks I'm being an idiot and trying to free Zandra in the dumbest way possible.

My second swing crashes through the lower portion of the six-foot-long steel bar. I grab it, use all my strength to work it free. Once done, I put the sword away, snatch the bar, and rush down the aisle toward the portal area.

Elizabeth turns at the sound of me running. For an instant, watching me charge in with a prison bar over my shoulder like a javelin makes her laugh. She stops finding it funny when I hurl my 'spear' at Azoth.

The front end passes harmlessly through the ninth-dimensional creature, gouges the concrete, and goes clattering into the hangar. Damn. So much for it sticking into the ground like an arrow and grounding the electrical being into oblivion. Elizabeth shakes her head at me, calling me an idiot with her facial expression.

Hmm.

When I spot some wiring dangling out of a maintenance hatch on the old cargo plane, I run for it. Elizabeth continues to watch me, much like a scientist observing rats. It only confuses her for a few seconds until she realizes—or reads it out of my head—I'm hoping the wires are still connected to batteries or something inside the plane capable of absorbing Azoth.

If he is a creature of pure electromagnetic energy, wires will suck him up like a vacuum hose… assuming they're connected to something like a capacitor on the other end.

Elizabeth objects to this plan.

How do I know this?

Because a huge stone stalagmite bursts out of the concrete in front of me, smashing into my gut like a hard punch from an earthen giant. Oof! When did this bitch learn elemental magic? The hit throws me backward into the air. I fly about fifteen feet before crashing flat on my back and sliding a bit more.

"I told you not to interfere," says Elizabeth in a stern tone.

"You did." I roll over into a push-up pose, and shove hard enough to launch myself upright. "I've never been very good at doing what I'm told, or what's logical, or safe… you should know that."

She folds her arms, moving to stand between me and Azoth. "For once, you should pretend not to hear that annoying little voice in your head telling you to get involved where you don't belong."

"You chose me for a reason. You could've gone after my sister."

"Or your daughter." Elizabeth smiles.

I narrow my eyes. Despite knowing she said that only to piss me off, I still get angry.

"Your sister lacks your nerve. She never would have been able to withstand the pressure of 'containing me' to save the world. Your daughter is too fearful, emotional, and lacking in self-control. She would've surrendered to me in a month." Elizabeth makes a face at me like I'm her pet dog who's wet the carpet for the fourth time in a week. "As much as you were my best option, your insufferable drive to help people is getting on my nerves. I thought we had an arrangement."

"We did… back when you planned on making a new reality out of thin air." I walk toward her, bracing a hand on my stomach where the rock lance hit me. Damn, that hurt… like running full speed into the end of a telephone pole. "You know me. Do you really think I'm going to stand idly by while you invade an alternate version of Earth to enslave all the people living there?"

She rolls her eyes. "I'm not going to *enslave* them. Far too much work to constantly put down insurrections. Why make slaves of them when terrifying them into obedience is so much less of a hassle?"

I stop almost within punching range of her. A bright violet energy field has started to appear inside the ring, growing inward. It's only about a quarter of the way done, but moving fast.

"What you're doing is evil."

"My dear, have you not been paying attention to anything these past few years?" Elizabeth chuckles. "What you call evil, I call the proper order of things. Look around you. Reality is 'evil.' Sentimentality and nobility are flaws of human construction. Do you consider wolves evil for consuming rabbits?"

"Neither wolves nor rabbits have the power to reason. You can find another way." I break to the left and charge at the stone ring.

It's only six inches thick. I can smash it.

Elizabeth catches up in a blur, grabbing me by the shoulder and belt. She drags me to a stop, then swings me to the side, tossing me across the hangar. I don't have time to even think about wings before I crash face-first into the old cargo plane, punching a hole in its fuselage like a Sam-shaped arrow. An explosion of dust fills the air around me from a pile of old canvas inside the plane.

Growling, I lurch to my feet, spit dust to the side, and stomp-kick the wall to make the hole bigger. A group of maybe a dozen other ascendant dark masters walks around the 'movie set' area, ignoring the mortal creators who have, for the most part, all crawled under their desks.

I jump out of the plane. Pale grey 'smoke' billows off my clothes as though I'd been dipped in flour. Again, I spit to the side.

The portal's about halfway done.

No way am I going to survive rushing into a group of ascendants plus Elizabeth. Need to smash the portal from a distance... but how. Frantic, I look around and spot a four-bladed propeller sitting on the floor below the engine it came from.

That works.

It's a bit unwieldy, but chucking a giant ninja star isn't *too* difficult when my target is a ten-foot-wide stone circle. I grab the propeller, spinning myself around a few times like I'm doing a hammer throw before letting it fly.

The enormous shuriken flies in a nasty curve. I frantically wave my arms to the left as if it will help.

It doesn't.

The propeller cruises on by, missing the stone circle by a wide margin and smacking into an enormous man who seriously looks like Viggo the Carpathian, barely moving him. Dude's gotta be almost eight feet tall. One prop blade impales him in the chest, leaving the entire propeller hanging from his body. He glances down at it, and sneers.

Oops. I offer a cheesy smile. "Sorry. Wasn't trying to hit you. There's a reason I never tried golf. Bit of a slice."

He snarls while pulling the propeller out.

The glowing field in the ring merges at the center. In an instant, what had been a curtain of purple light shifts, becoming an open hole to dense jungle. The scenery doesn't look the least bit strange, so it's unclear if I'm seeing somewhere else on this Earth or another world entirely. However, Azoth said they couldn't hop sideways into another dimension from here, so it has to be Earth. Perhaps even a place with intersecting ley lines.

Big guy tries to throw the prop at me, but it swerves wildly upward and smashes through the ceiling with a loud clamor of metal crashing into metal… and probably lands a ways off outside. The hole in his chest begins to close fast enough to see with the naked eye. Still growling at me, he shakes his head and walks into the gateway.

So weird. Why aren't they all coming after me at once? Oh… wait. They're vulnerable and they know it. If they die in this form, they're gone for good. No connection to the Void means they're metaphorically pants-down right now. Even if they believe themselves more powerful than me, none of them want to risk being the one unlucky bastard I take down before they overwhelm me.

More ascendant dark masters hurry in. Damn! I really need to close this freakin' gate.

Time to charge.

Elizabeth intercepts, dashing in front of me while summoning a scimitar out of thin air. I reflexively yank the Devil Killer out of its dimensional pocket, swinging it up in time to block. Our blades cross for an instant, mine spitting ember sparks where the steel scrapes. Her sword appears Persian, dark Damascus steel, thin glowing green markings along the handguard. I don't have time to admire it; she shoves me back. This time, I manage to stay on my feet.

She lunges in, slicing for my gut. I turn her attack, our blades scraping as I redirect her weapon to the side, spin, and stab at her. For some stupid reason, I try to be nice and aim for her leg instead of a vital area.

Three inches of the Devil Killer's tip sink into her thigh, leaving a smoking wound. She screams like I burned her with a red-hot iron, catching me with a back-handed sword punch across the jaw so damn fast it looked like a blur to me despite being a vampire.

I land ten feet away on my face. Yeah. Jaw's probably busted. Owie.

More worrisome is Elizabeth not making a snide remark or taunt. Certain she's coming to finish me off, I spring to my feet and round my sword to parry the expected attack. Apparently, sharing head space with her for so long paid off: she swings exactly where I thought she would. However, she's freakin' *fast*. She redirects her strike around my defense, landing a nice slash down the outside of my left arm.

Beats having my head cut off.

Except… the slash *burns* like she's poured acid in it. Actually, I think she technically *did* put acid in it, at least, if the smoke means anything.

I'm screaming before I realize it.

Laughing, Elizabeth presses the attack, trying to take advantage of my surprise at feeling so much pain from a relatively shallow flesh wound. I catch her blade with mine, pivot, and ram myself into her, body to body, knocking her flying.

She hits the ground tumbling into a logroll, but she's back on her feet before I'm close enough to get a free hit, swatting my thrust aside and slashing back at me so rapidly I have no choice but to fling myself over backward to avoid her slicing me in half at the waist. She spins from the force she put behind the strike, almost losing her balance. I kick my legs up, briefly doing a handstand before flipping upright again.

Somewhere behind us, dozens of ascendant dark masters rush through the portal.

Elizabeth comes at me like a bladed dervish. She's moving faster than Sebastian, but not by *too* much. However, he's quite obviously more skilled. In fact, it feels like I'm an even match or modestly better than her in terms of technique. Again and again, our blades ring off each other. The stinging pain in my arm finally stops after about a minute.

Frustration shows on her face. Guess she hasn't been spying on me as much as I thought or she'd know I've been training pretty intensively with Sebastian since returning from Europe. Maybe I *do* have a little bit of pride after all, since getting my butt kicked by freakin' zombie Vikings annoyed me.

If she wasn't so much faster than me, I'd have ended this fight in about eighteen seconds. Probably longer since I'd been trying *not* to kill her... but she's rapidly backing me into a corner where it seems I have no other choice. Yeah, I know. Being dumb. Stupid sentimentality. I need to stop hesitating.

She finally commits a mistake, overextending herself when I pretend to miscalculate—but rather than leave my chest open, I swing the Devil Killer down in a circular arc, catching her sword and sweeping it up over her head. A little twist of my wrists throws her weapon from her grip.

I point the Devil Killer at her face. "Call them back."

Elizabeth thrusts her hand at me.

Invisible force like a speeding city bus crashes into me, throwing me halfway across the hangar. The whole world spins in a disorienting blur. I focus so much on preventing the magical blast from stripping my sword from my grip that I have nothing left for balance and end up on my ass again.

Elizabeth summons her sword and is in my face again, swinging down at my head. I block, but she's got the advantage of standing over me while I'm sprawled on the floor. Sparks fly from where the edges of our swords cross, spewing hot orange rain. My jeans ignite in several spots.

"*Aistiraha!*" rasps Elizabeth in a deep, polyphonic voice like three of her speaking at once.

My left arm abruptly breaks halfway between shoulder and elbow.

Screaming past clenched teeth, I struggle to

hold her blade away from my face with my remaining arm. The acidic scimitar inches closer. I stare into her eyes, knowing she's about to use the same spell again to snap the bone in my right arm.

This is it...

Guess she wasn't afraid of me after all.

A sudden, weird urge hits me out of nowhere.

I extend the wings Azrael gave me.

Elizabeth grins. *"Aist—"*

My wings ignite in a flash of golden brilliance, flames as bright as sunlight.

Elizabeth's face blackens in seconds. Shrieking, she jumps back from me. The sudden loss of pressure on my arm causes me to nearly throw the Devil Killer up over my head. My wings give off a giant beam like a searchlight. I raise them, bending the tips in to focus on her.

She screams, shielding her face with her arms and backing off.

Ooo-kay. This is new. Not gonna look a gift horse in the mouth, though.

I drag myself onto my feet and stalk toward her, focusing on her mental energy and feeding. A firehose of power floods my consciousness, tingling in my sinuses. I go from weary to over-caffeinated in seconds.

Elizabeth thrusts her left hand at me, rasping indecipherably foreign words.

A pool of inky blackness spreads over the floor outward from where I'm standing. Uh oh. It's probably a real bad idea to stand on this stuff. I abandon trying to psychically vampirize Elizabeth into a comatose state and leap into flight. Dozens of tentacles shoot up from the void and wrap around my legs, pinning them together. I raise the sword to slash at them, but the mass of slimy appendages begins swinging me around.

"I'm afraid I can't waste any more time with you," wheezes Elizabeth. "Enjoy the elder horror."

I keep trying to slash at the mass of darkness trying to engulf me while the smoking bitch sprints away toward the creators' cells. The instant I sever the first tentacle, the others holding me go berserk. Up, down, and sideways lose meaning. The creature whips me back and forth, pounding my body into the concrete floor over and over again at both ends of an agony rainbow.

Zandra screams.

Growling, I flap my wings with all the strength I can muster to stop this damned thing from breaking every bone in my body. Pain like the wings are going to tear from my back makes me scream in anger, but I manage to stop myself from kissing the floor again. Hovering gives me a moment to look toward the cell area. Multiple black tentacles have erupted from the floor all over the place, including all throughout the 'movie set' of fake offices. One's grabbed Zandra, holding her off the ground.

"No, you fool!" shouts Elizabeth at the creature. "Not that one. I comm—oh, forget it." She gestures in the general direction of the cells. All the doors swing open, unlocked.

I grab the tentacle around my waist. It's too slimy to get a grip on, so I extend my claws and sink them in.

Lance, Quentin, and Ramani walk out of their cells like robots and hurry toward Elizabeth.

"Stop!" I stare at Lance, trying to give him a mental command to obey me.

I'd have better luck trying to get four-year-old Anthony to eat broccoli.

Lance Blackburn completely ignores me and walks through the shimmering gate, Ramani and Quentin right behind him.

Another tentacle wraps around my neck.

Zandra's tentacle rears back, about to smash her into the floor.

Elizabeth hurries for the portal, which is already starting to close. If I teleport into the air above her, I might be able to take her head off before she sees me coming, stopping her from getting away—but Zandra is seconds from death. Going after Elizabeth means an innocent woman dies.

Shit! Fuck it. I can't let that thing kill Zandra.

I teleport the hundred or so yards to her and slash the tentacle at the base before it can pound her face-first into the concrete floor. She drops to all fours, tangled in the dead, fleshy tube. I pivot, intending to teleport after Elizabeth—but the gateway's gone. The stone ring is merely a bizarre art object. No portal. Not even a single spark of lightning.

Dammit. I sigh, hanging my head. All those people in that other world…

"I am never…" Zandra coughs, pushing her way free. "*Never* having tako again."

A tentacle from the hallway outside the cell reaches in to grab me. I casually slice it out of the air, barely looking at it. "How can you live in California and not eat tacos?"

"No, my dear." She shifts sideways and sits on the rug. "Tako, as in octopus sushi."

"Oh, yeah. Agreed." I narrow my eyes at the

main blob sprouting tentacles and tighten my grip on the Devil Killer. "Speaking of sushi… be right back."

Chapter Twenty-Five
Side-Skipping Dimensions

For something called an elder horror, the mass of tentacles died fairly easily.

Much easier to fight one when it can't reach you. I decided to stay out of its range and pepper it with the little witchy energy bolts Allison taught me. Took about a dozen of them to blast the monstrosity back into a vaporous cloud. By the time I finished doing it, the overabundance of energy I'd absorbed from Elizabeth had once again given way to me feeling hungry. Well, tired. These days, tired and hungry are the same thing.

"Well, that could've gone better," I say, glancing at Tyson's remains. "I'm sorry. I shouldn't have trusted her promise none of you would be hurt."

"What happened to him hadn't been in her plan," says Zandra.

I sigh at the Devil Killer in my hand. What kind of moron am I to sit down at a table with Elizabeth and believe her?

"She definitely did not anticipate this." Zandra walks up to me, the scuff of her shoes on concrete echoing over the now-silent hangar. "She wanted us to create an entirely new world for her. I'm sure what she told you about taking the dark masters with her was true. But we couldn't do it. In those few moments we linked with the alien, it felt as though many days passed. We couldn't create a fully-fleshed-out world on a planetary scale. At least, not that quickly."

"Maybe you couldn't, but she seemed to believe Azoth could bring it all together." I grumble and put the Devil Killer back in its pocket dimension.

"The problem is... most of the people living in the reality we'd have produced would have been like background extras in a movie, mere scenery. Any person we didn't specifically write about would be generic and, according to Elizabeth, 'unfulfilling' to rule over. She required genuine people with genuine souls to dominate. Mannequins pretending to be commoners cowering from her 'awesome power' would not have satisfied her."

"Sick bitch."

Zandra chuckles. "Perhaps a bit coarser than I'd have put it, but yes. Essentially."

"I'm guessing Azoth tried dragging information about humans out of you in order to give billions of people enough detail to bring them to life… and Tyson overloaded."

"More than Tyson. We all did." She rubs her forehead. "I'm going to have this migraine for weeks. I do believe Tyson's sudden explosion triggered a feedback wave powerful enough to stun the alien before he killed all of us. Ty's death saved us, though I doubt he intended to sacrifice himself on purpose."

"I shouldn't have even talked to her. Should have just gone straight to the swordfight."

Zandra rests her hand on my arm. "Don't blame yourself, dear. Even angels have their limits."

"I'm not really an angel. I just play one on TV."

She tilts her head.

"It's a long, complicated story… probably fill up like eighteen books."

Zandra brushes her fingertips down my wing. "Well, you're an angel as far as I'm concerned. You sure heard my prayers."

"Actually, Greta hired me."

"What?"

"I'm a private investigator. Neither she nor I had any idea how weird your disappearance would get. I thought it would be an ordinary abduction... not freakin' Elizabeth finally making her move."

"I get the feeling you and this woman have some history."

"Heh. Yeah... had a couple bad years where I just couldn't get her out of my mind."

"That had to be rough."

I give her a 'you have no idea' side-eye glance.

"What is she? Clearly not a normal person."

"Short answer is: a powerful vampire. Longer answer is: they are ancient, powerful sorcerers who escaped the cycle of reincarnation, but were banished to the Void thanks to a war instigated by her son against his own mother. They found a loophole out of the Void by possessing certain humans, resulting in their becoming creatures like vampires, werewolves, and so on."

"Oh. I always did suspect such beings were

real." She smiles. "Never saw one before, but I made a career of reading about strange things, looking for story inspiration, you see. Some stuff out there is quite difficult to explain unless you keep an open mind to supernatural things being real."

"Yeah." I run a hand down my face. "Did you happen to get any idea where Elizabeth went?"

She closes her eyes, straining to concentrate. After a moment, she exhales, looks at me. "I'm sorry. All I can tell you is that I saw many landscapes. Deserts, lush forests, mountains, people riding upon giant birds, tribal warriors running through the woods. A hundred momentary flashes from different worlds. She could have gone to any of them."

"Azoth said they couldn't step sideways from here." I point at the stone ring. "So they had to go somewhere else in this world first. I saw jungle through the portal."

"You know, I vaguely remember while we were in the trance… it would have been barely a second before we exploded, but it felt like hours. Though he appeared to understand we would fail, he kept trying to pull more and more information out of us. But at the same time, he also got the idea to send Elizabeth to a parallel dimension on this level. Do you know what that means?"

"Unfortunately, I do."

"What does it mean?"

I give her a brief explanation about there being a hundred dimensions stacked on top of each other, the Source of all creation being the 100th dimension at the top. Within each level, a theoretically infinite number of parallel dimensions can stretch out 'sideways'. There could be millions and millions of Earth-like realities all occupying the third dimension.

She whistles. "It's going to take me a while to process that."

"Did the alien think about where he might have needed to go in order to open a gateway to a specific place?"

"Hmm. I think he said something about needing a huge ley line nexus." She waves dismissively. "The creature seemed to be able to do nine thousand things at once and spent 8,500 of his consciousness threads complaining about how primitive this world was because he couldn't simply make doorways wherever he wanted."

I pick at my slashed shirt sleeve. At least the cut on my arm is closed. "Yeah, to him, working here had to be like asking a group of NASA scientists to build a space shuttle using only an abacus and bamboo."

She chuckles.

"Umm." I point at the ring again. "If he couldn't simply open portals anywhere he wanted, why did Elizabeth bother making this ring here?"

"It would have worked if the five of us established in the lore of our created world that the ring gate worked. That's the beauty of dealing with a reality we're creating from scratch."

"Ah, okay. Hmm, I ran into a creator awhile back. Charlie Reed."

"Oh, yes. The *Dur* books." Zandra grins. "I loved those."

"I wound up inside his world for a little while. How did he pull that off, but this failed?"

Zandra shrugs. "Off the top of my head, I'd say because you were there only for a limited time, probably just the part of events he'd written specifically about. Elizabeth wanted us to create a permanent living world, not merely a story-length feature."

"Oh."

Zandra looks around at the hangar. "I don't suppose you'd mind giving me a lift home? Or at least to the airport?"

"Sure. Your daughter hiring me to find you

is the reason I'm here, after all. Least I can do is get you back to her."

"Thank you, dear. Are you parked close? Or did you fly here?"

"Yes and no." I take her hand. "Brace yourself, it's a little chilly out."

Chapter Twenty-Six
A Simple Explanation

Appearing outside behind the East Coast Pizza building in an instant startles a gasp from Zandra.

Or maybe the negative thirty-degree temperature did that.

Tammy, Anthony, and Allison are already out there waiting for me since my daughter had been watching me. As soon as the teleport finishes, she grabs me and starts crying. I don't have to ask why she's emotional... she saw Elizabeth's sword come within inches of my face. One arm-breaking spell away from the end. Speaking of which, the broken arm is going to be tender for an hour or so. Allison enchants Zandra to be resistant to the cold.

We all hold hands, and I teleport us directly to my living room. I collect the ashtray/coaster/figurine, then teleport again with Zandra directly to her house.

Some aspects of the events in Barrow, Alaska, I'm going to leave in Zandra's head. She's in the unique position of being a B-list director, so if she starts rambling on about vampires and portals and aliens, people are going to think she's finally gone loopy. Also, she's a creator who's up to her eyeballs in this mess. It wouldn't be fair to leave her defenseless against any retaliation from Elizabeth.

I do, however, give her a false memory of flying back here in another small private jet. Probably silly and extra of me, but the fewer people who know teleportation is a thing, the better.

While she stands there in a daze from the memory alteration, I replace the weird object on her desk and call Greta to let her know I've brought her mother home. She—understandably—flips out, starts demanding details, then asks me to wait there before hanging up.

Sigh. Kind of in a hurry here... but okay.

Upon hearing her daughter is on the way, Zandra rushes off to shower and change as she's been wearing the same clothes since her abduction. So strange to see this woman who came within inches of death treating the entire experience as an adventure.

About twenty minutes later, Greta runs in the door shouting for her mother.

"She's cleaning up. Give her a few minutes. She's had a rough time."

"What hap—?"

Zandra, in a loose top and long skirt that makes her look like a new-age fortuneteller, breezes into the room and embraces her daughter. "There you are."

"Mom!" Greta, seemingly stunned at her mother's blasé reaction, stares at us, lost for words.

"I'll leave you two to your privacy. Need to go find you-know-who," I say, edging for the door.

"Wait. You never told me what your fee is," says Greta.

"Forget it. Finding your mother ended up being part of another case I've already paid for."

Zandra blinks at me. "Don't you mean *been* paid for?"

"No, not really." I laugh. "Still paying for it. It's fine. Your mother is safe."

"Who took her?" asks Greta, almost yelling.

"It's a really long, complicated story you'd never believe," I say.

"Try me." She puts her hands on her hips.

"Okay..." I give her a 'you asked for it' look. "A powerful ancient sorceress who's become an immortal being of darkness tried to create a new universe by forcing your mother plus several other people with the power to create alternate realities to write about it, but it didn't work. The whole thing collapsed in on itself and failed."

Greta regards me for a long moment, then starts lightly shaking her head. "You aren't old enough to be senile. You sound like Mom, but at least I know she's talking about weird movies."

"I am not senile." Zandra holds her chin up.

I smile, somewhat patronizingly, at Greta, and make her forget me saying that. As far as she knows, her mother was picked up accidentally by a car service looking for someone else and drove her halfway across the country before they figured out the mistake.

Greta stares into space as her brain processes the new memory.

"Did you do something to my daughter? Why does she look stoned?" Zandra waves her hand by Greta's eyes to no reaction.

"I gave your daughter an alternate version of events. She thinks a car service picked you up by mistake because you looked like the person they needed to drive to Florida. If you want to tell her the truth, be my guest. Sorry, but I can't waste too much time having a pointless argument with her about reality. I have to find Elizabeth before she invades some other dimension."

Zandra chuckles. "Greta always did lack imagination. She'll be happier with a simple explanation. Thank you, dear." She hugs me with copious back-patting. "Now go stop that bitch."

"On it." I wish her luck and head out the door.

Time to teleport home… after I find some people to feed from. I'm so hungry I could eat an entire mall.

Chapter Twenty-Seven
All Culty and Weird

As soon as I reappear in my living room, Tammy and Allison mob me.

My daughter's still a little clingy after watching me almost die. Or at least suffer a major head wound. I calm her by saying Elizabeth couldn't have killed me. Slicing my head in half would have only knocked me out until my vampiric healing kicked in.

Of course, since she can see into my head, she finds my little nugget of doubt. After all, I still don't know for a fact what will happen if I suffer a wound ordinarily fatal to a human. For that matter, I'm unsure if my body *is* technically alive or merely much better at faking it.

She calms a bit, but remains nervous.

The four of us discuss the events of the hangar and where Elizabeth might have gone. Allison starts rambling about ley line nexuses in jungles. She knows *of* ley lines but never bothered studying them since our witchcraft methodology doesn't make too much use of them. Some shamanistic or animistic occultists *need* them. As in, the closer they are to a ley line, the more powerful they get... and if they're nowhere near one, they have almost no magic at all.

Sucks to be them, right?

Of course, on a nexus they'd be ridiculously powerful. Guess it's a tradeoff. Truth be told, I had my fair share of dealing with ley lines during the Civil War. They're powerful and they work.

Anyway, after about twenty minutes of debate, I make a reluctant decision.

"Tam, can you try to locate her?"

"No way," says Anthony. "Opening her mind to Elizabeth could be... bad."

"I agree with the human fart machine." Allison points at him.

Anthony reddens, stands a little straighter. Yeah, he's crushing hard.

I close my eyes, sighing. "Okay, forget it.

He's right. Bad idea. I'll find another way."

"She's in Venezuela." Tammy gazes up at the ceiling, her faerie amulet dangling on its cord from her fingers. As in *not* being worn. Her overly casual demeanor abruptly crashes into an expression of horrified shock. "Oh, *gawd*. They've got a bunch of people tied up to trees. The big, creepy vamps are wearing robes. Eww. It's all culty and weird. Elizabeth is there and she's—*eek!*" She hastily pulls the amulet on, keeping both hands clamped over it for extra protection.

I grasp her shoulders, staring into her eyes... worry makes my heart pound. "What? What's wrong?"

She swallows hard. "She looked right at me, err the person whose mind I hopped into. But I'm fine. Just shook me." My daughter takes a few more breaths. "Yeah, that was terrifying. Okay, she's in Venezuela and they're going to kill those people to open the gate."

"Oh, shit," mutters Anthony.

I pull out my phone with one hand, pointing at him with the other. "Curse word excused. Allowable use."

"What's the plan?" asks Allison.

"Sec." I dial Kingsley and Max at the same time, threading the calls into a conference.

"Samantha?" asks Max, answering first. "What are you doing back in California? We are almost ready to leave for Alaska."

"Oh, Sam," says Kingsley. "Good timing. I was thinking tonight, you might want to put on —"

"Kingsley! Not now. You're on speakerphone. Max, Kingsley, guys... we need to go to Venezuela. *Now.*"

"Oh, no. Not another vacation," groans Kingsley.

"No," I say, shaking my head. "Far from a vacation. Elizabeth is down there preparing a ritual to sacrifice a bunch of people to open a door into a parallel dimension she intends to invade."

Tammy gives me a fearful look. "And I think she knows we're coming."

"Yeah. Probably." I exhale hard. "But she's also overconfident."

"So, ixnay on Alaska?" says the Alchemist.

"Definitely ixnay."

"So, what's the plan, Sam?" asks Max.

"The plan is to get to Venezuela as fast as we can and stop her from doing whatever she's doing any way we can," I say.

Kingsley exhales. "Please tell me you have something more than a high school football coach's pep talk. What exactly are we going to do?"

"We're not even entirely sure what we're dealing with yet." A soft tingle caresses my back, making me smile to myself. "Pretty sure I'm going to have to wing it."

The End

~~~~~

To be continued in:
Infinite Moon
Vampire for Hire #20
Available now!

About J.R. Rain:

J.R. Rain is an ex-private investigator who now writes full-time. He lives in a small house on a small island with his small dog, Sadie. Please visit him at www.jrrain.com.

About Matthew S. Cox:

Originally from South Amboy NJ, **Matthew S. Cox** has been creating science fiction and fantasy worlds for most of his reasoning life. Since 1996, he has developed the "Divergent Fates" world, in which Division Zero, Virtual Immortality, The Awakened Series, The Harmony Paradox, and the Daughter of Mars series take place.

Matthew is an avid gamer, a recovered WoW addict, Gamemaster for two custom systems, and a fan of anime, British humour, and intellectual science fiction that questions the nature of reality, life, and what happens after it.

He is also fond of cats.

Please find him at: www.matthewcoxbooks.com

Printed in Great Britain
by Amazon